THE MIDNIGHT HUNT

RITE WORLD: LIGHTGROVE WITCHES
BOOK 5

JULIANA HAYGERT

COPYRIGHT

This book is a work of fiction. Names, characters, places, and incidents either are products of the author's imagination or are used fictitiously. Any resemblance to actual persons, living or dead, events, or locales is entirely coincidental.

Copyright © 2023 by Juliana Haygert

All rights reserved. This book or any portion thereof may not be reproduced or used in any manner whatsoever without the express written permission of the publisher except for the use of brief quotations in a book review.

Manufactured in the United States of America.

First Edition April 2023

Edited by H. Danielle Crabtree

Proofreading by Kimberly Cannon

Cover design by Moonchildljilja

Any trademark, service marks, product names, or names featured are the property of their respective owners, and are used only for reference. There is no implied endorsement if one of these terms is used.

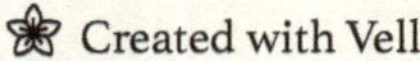 Created with Vellum

RITE WORLD

Welcome to the RITE WORLD!

For a printable reading order, click here!

Free Novellas:
The Vampire Hunt
The Light Witch

Novellas:
The Hunter Path
The Light Calling
The Light Witch
The Wicked Alliance
The Shadow Fae

The Fae Queen

Rite World:
The Vampire Heir (Book 1)
The Witch Queen (Book 2)
The Immortal Vow (Book 3)
The Warlock Lord (Book 4)
The Wolf Consort (Book 5)
The Crystal Rose (Book 6)
The Wolf Forsaken (Book 7)
The Fae Bound (Book 8)
The Blood Pact (Book 9)

Rite World: Blackthorn Hunters Academy
The Demons Kiss (Book 1)
The Hunter Secret (Book 2)
The Soul Bond (Book 3)
The Shadow Trials (Book 4)
The Immortal Vow (Book 5)

Rite World: Vampire Wars
The Darkest Vampire (Book 1)
The Darkest Witch (Book 2)
The Darkest Magic (Book 3)

Rite World: Night Wolves
The Night Calling (Book 1)
The Night Burning (Book 2)
The Night Hunting (Book 3)
The Night Rising (Book 4)

Rite World: Lightgrove Witches
The Midnight Test (Book 1)
The Midnight Spell (Book 2)
The Midnight Flame (Book 3)
The Midnight Secret (Book 4)
The Midnight Hunt (Book 5)
The Midnight Wish (Book 6)

And more to come!

AUTHOR'S NOTE

I hope you enjoy reading *The Midnight Hunt*!

Don't forget to sign up for my Newsletter to find out about new releases, cover reveals, giveaways, and more!

If you want to see exclusive teasers, help me decide on covers, read excerpts, talk about books, etc, join my reader group on Facebook: Juliana's Club!

DISCLAIMER

This is a work of fiction in the fantasy genre. Because of that, I took the liberty of creating a country in Europe that never existed (think like The Princess Diaries and Genovia) for our heroine's backstory. Some towns in Germany and Italy are also fictitious. Despite that, I hope you like this story! :)

1

My mind was in a daze. I barely registered as the sisters created a heavy mist around us, and rushed me and Shade, who was still inside the cage, out of the parking lot. We ran for a few minutes, my heart pounding against my breastbone. Anna shoved me in the backseat of a car, while Britta freed the black cat from the metal crate.

I stared at Shade's limp form in Britta's hands.

That was my familiar.

Shouldn't I feel him?

Did that mean he was dead? Or was it because our connection hadn't been restored yet?

I shook my head, my thoughts confused, my head hurting.

Anna slipped into the driver's seat, while Britta sat in the passenger's, still cradling Shade like a porcelain doll. Anna didn't waste a second—the moment Britta's feet were inside, she peeled away.

"Watch it," Britta grumbled as she had to pull the door hard to close it with the car moving.

For a moment, the car was so quiet, I didn't have any choice but to drown in my own thoughts. Holy shit, what had happened? Grace and Starla were dark witches, but they weren't evil. The queen of the Darkmist coven had killed them. The Darkmist queen had done something to Sean, and now Sean wasn't himself.

And Shade lay immobile in Britta's lap.

I opened my mouth to ask if he was okay, but before I could, Britta hovered her hands over his body and faint while light shone from her palms. She closed her eyes and whispered something I couldn't hear.

A few seconds later, Shade inhaled deeply and his chest started moving. He let out a soft meow.

A sob lodged in my throat.

As if the sound had snapped her barely controlled rage, Anna glared at me over her shoulder. "What the hell were you thinking?" She faced the front again, but she kept staring at me through the rearview mirror, her eyes cold. She gripped the wheel until her knuckles turned white. "You could have gotten yourself killed!"

"Anna," Britta called. "Stop it. Focus on the road. We need to get out of here." She looked at me, disappointment written all over her face. "We can talk about this later."

Another sob rose, but this time, I didn't try to hide it. I settled back in the seat and glanced out the window as the night rushed past us, my eyes unseeing. Tears rolled down my cheeks and sadness filled my chest.

This wasn't how things were supposed to be.

I DIDN'T PAY ATTENTION TO THE DIRECTION ANNA WAS driving. At some point, I fell asleep from pure exhaustion and woke when Britta touched my shoulder. It took me a second to remember everything, and then I wanted to close my eyes and go to sleep again, pretend nothing was happening.

"Come on," Britta said, her voice an inch gentler than before. "You need proper rest."

I scooted out of the car and stared at the rundown roadside inn in front of us as Anna marched inside the reception. Movement to my right caught my attention and I turned. I stared, stunned, at Shade, now in his human form. He leaned on the side of the car, his clothes rumpled, his hair messy, and his face full of tiny cuts and purpling wounds.

"Shade," I whispered, taking a step toward him.

He straightened, as if he didn't like being seen in this state. "I'm fine." His voice was rough and shallow. "I'll be fine."

I didn't know what to do. Should I apologize for not following the sisters' plan, or simply for being unlucky?

Saving me from my misery, Anna emerged from inside the inn, irritation noticeable in every one of her movements. She showed us two cards. "Let's get inside."

"Wait," Britta said. She touched the car, and it changed from a dark red to a light blue and the plate to another state. "We can't be sure the mist confused them all and no one saw us."

She and Anna took the lead, and Shade and I followed. I frowned as we climbed the outside stairs, thinking about the mist. So, it wasn't just the other witches couldn't see it. It made them confused so they couldn't follow us.

Genius.

The mist, healing Shade, changing the car—the sisters were more powerful than I realized.

Anna turned a corner and stopped in front of the two side-by-side doors. "I made sure to pick adjoining rooms with no guests right beside or under us."

I wanted to ask her how, but I knew she had spelled the receptionist. The poor person probably wouldn't even remember renting these two rooms.

She slid the card into the card reader and pushed the door open. We entered the room—a short hallway with a door to the bathroom and a small closet and counter with the coffee machine, and two queen beds. Tacky carpets, heavy curtains, and bedding that looked straight out of the last century. I bet it smelled like it too.

To the side, another door connected to the second room.

Groaning, Shade plopped down on one of the beds, and the sisters and I stood there, staring at each other.

"Now you can yell at her," Britta said.

Anna turned her burning gaze at me. She hadn't stopped glaring since they arrived in the school's parking lot and saved Shade and me, but now her frown deepened.

"I don't even know what to say," Anna said through gritted teeth. "I thought you were smarter than this."

I stilled. "Did you really think I would stay behind and leave Sean and Shade in Grace's clutches?"

"Grace isn't as bad as you thought," Anna barked. Then she sobered up. "Wasn't."

"I didn't know that, and I think you didn't either."

"That's not the point!" Anna yelled.

"Then what is the point?" I barked, my voice rising.

Anna clasped my shoulders and fixed her eyes on mine. "You're too important, Hazel. The most important witch alive right now. We can't lose you, no matter the consequences."

I stepped back and out of her reach. "I won't let other people, especially people I love, get hurt for my own sake." I sucked in a sharp inhale as something else came to mind. "My mother, my sister. Catarina and her witches might go after them, use them to get to me."

"Shit." Britta pulled out her phone from her pocket. "I'll ask someone to check on them, make sure they are okay. If they are, we'll get them into hiding."

I frowned. "Someone?"

"We have a few allies here and there," Anna explained.

"My mother and my sister won't go with strangers," I said.

"You can talk to them on the phone," Britta said, the phone already pressed against her ear. "But do not tell them who you are. Not yet. It'll put them at risk. Hello?" She turned her back to us and started talking in another language. Was that Greek?

Anna pointed her finger at my face. "You're not off the hook."

I seethed. "You're supposed to be one of my best friends, but you're acting like my freaking mother."

"Well, you're acting like a child!"

"What?" I squealed.

"For the light's sake," Shade groaned. He sat up in bed and stared at the both of us. "Can you two shut up? I'm tired and dizzy, and your nonsense is making my head hurt."

I shrank into myself. "Sorry."

Anna crossed her arms and huffed. Who was the child now?

"Besides, no one is right or wrong here," he said. "The past is the past; we can't change what happened. We can only try to do better in the future."

I raised my eyebrows at him. I didn't remember much about him and I hadn't known him long in this life, but I knew Shade wasn't the philosophical type.

I sat beside him. "Can you tell us what happened, or do you want to rest first and we can talk tomorrow morning?"

"It's already tomorrow." He gestured to the clock on the nightstand—it read three twenty-six in the morning. "And I can tell you now, I'm tired and hurting, but too worked up to sleep yet."

Britta finished her call, her eyes finding me immediately. "Our friend is packing to go see your mother and sister. She'll arrive mid-morning, then she'll call you so you can talk to them. Hopefully, they will listen to you."

"Hopefully." I had to think what I was going to say. My mother idolized the Lightgrove witches. She wouldn't back down from any threat related to the coven.

"If they don't go willingly, my friend can enchant them. I promise it won't hurt them."

I didn't like that, but what other choice did I have?

"Thanks," I muttered, then turned to Shade. "Tell us."

He let out a long sigh. "It all went well at the beginning. Fast and easy. Sean and I went to your dorm, used your key, grabbed most of your things, then we went to his apartment, got his things. I mean, he was getting his things, I was browsing Netflix."

"Of course," Anna said.

"On the way back, a force slammed into the car and pushed us off the road, just outside of town," he continued. "I was driving, and I hit my head on the steering wheel." He pressed a hand to a small cut above his eyebrow. "I was dizzy and barely registered what was happening. The witches surrounded us and used their magic before we could do anything." His brows curled down. "I didn't see anything—their vehicles, where they took us. All I remember was that every hour or so they withdrew their magic. We were in a dark room with gray walls, our wrists and ankles chained to hooks on the floor." He showed us his wrists, where the cuffs had left red marks. He looked at me. "They wanted to know where you were hiding, what you knew, and what your plans were. Sean and I remained quiet, even through their torture."

I winced.

Britta sat on the bed behind Shade and hovered her hands over his back. He glanced at her. "Just relax. I'm going to check if anything is too damaged and try to heal you as much as I can." Faint white light shone from her palms and Shade let out a soft sigh.

"Anyway." He cleared his throat. "We just endured it."

My brows slammed down. "I'm sorry this happened to you."

He shrugged. "Part of the job, I guess."

My familiar—Arianna's familiar—shouldn't have to come with a warning label.

"Better?" Britta asked Shade. He nodded and she got up from the bed. "That's enough for one night. We need to rest. Let's sleep for a handful of hours and then continue moving."

"Where are we going?" I asked. I knew we had to hide in a better place.

"I don't know," she said, worrying her lower lip with her teeth. "But we'll figure it out."

Anna opened the connecting door and the sisters walked into the second room.

I stood from beside Shade and moved to the other bed. I took off my shoes, my jacket, and lay down in bed. I was tired, hungry, and hurt, but I doubted I could fall sleep right now, either.

But I had to at least try.

2

I WAS WRONG.

I slept like a rock. When Shade shook me awake around nine in the morning, I was so out of it, I couldn't remember anything. Then it all came slamming into me, and I had to force myself to breathe, to stay calm.

Holy shit. I couldn't believe everything that had happened in the last couple of days: Grace revealing she was a dark witch, becoming a fugitive among the light witches, meeting Anna and Britta, learning I was the reincarnation of Arianna, the greatest light witch of all time.

But things really spiraled out of control when I defied the sisters and met Grace last night.

And now Sean was … I didn't even know what he was.

A pang cut through my heart. No, I couldn't let that get me down. I couldn't just give in and sulk. There had to be a way of bringing him back, and I would find it.

"Let's go," Anna snapped when she came into my room. Apparently, she was still mad at me.

Hell, I was still mad at myself, though when I thought about it, I didn't see myself doing anything different.

After grabbing a quick breakfast at a local McDonald's drive-thru, we drove. Shade was behind the wheel, and he drove mostly in circles. We went to one town, stopped, one of the sisters changed the car's color and plates, and then we moved on to the next town, always within a three-hour radius of New Orleans.

If the sisters had their way, we would leave the area, but the Lightgrove coven was in New Orleans, along with all of our problems. We could run away for a while, but not for long.

Late morning, I got news from my mother and Amanda. Apparently, my mother had freaked out when the witch tried talking to them about the situation. She screamed at the top of her lungs, so the witch spelled them both. Right now, they were like dolls in the backseat of a car, being taken north to only the light knew where. Apprehension took hold of my heart, but I chose to trust Anna and Britta. They had never let me down, not in this life, not in the previous one. I felt guilty for doing this to my mother and sister, but it was that or ... I couldn't even think about it.

"They will be fine," Britta assured me. She reached across the backseat and held my hand in hers. "They might not have a lot of power, but they are smart."

"I—" I closed my mouth as an image flashed in my mind.

I was seated at a crude wooden table, working on embroi-

dery. I wore a simple light blue dress, and had my long, blond hair in a loose braid behind my back.

A young girl walked behind me. She put plates and utensils on the table, and then I saw the older woman in front of a steaming pot over a fire.

She reached inside the pot with a long wooden spoon, scooped some of the soup, blew on it, then tried it. She smiled and looked at me. "It's good. Just the way you like it."

I gasped and blinked, suddenly back in the moving car.

"Sweet potato and rosemary soup," I whispered. Yes, my favorite back then, but more shocking than that was the fact that my mother and my sister were there. "They look exactly the same."

Britta tilted her head. "What did you see?"

"My mother and sister."

She nodded. "Oh, yes."

"How is that possible?"

"We believe that some people around you are the same ones from before," she explained. "Like Thales. And your mother and sister. And probably some other people you haven't recognize yet. They all reincarnated with you."

My brows curled down. "But my mother was born before me."

"The universe was already getting ready for you."

Why? Why me? Was I that special? What had I done that deserved such privilege? I didn't feel so good about this.

We drove around the entire day. It was late at night when we finally reached the place Anna had found online —a cute lodge with cabins spread out over a large hill two hours from New Orleans. She had booked one large cabin with a fake name and ID. The best thing was that everything was done online. We didn't see anyone as we crossed the gates and drove the narrow gravel path toward the cabins.

The path forked every so often and a sign indicated the cabin names each path led to.

I didn't know if she had done it on purpose, but our cabin was on the other side of the hill, deep in the trees. As we exited the car, I inhaled the fresh air and I could believe we were really in the middle of nowhere.

"We should be safe here," Anna said as she opened the trunk and grabbed a duffel bag. Two of our stops had been to a Walmart and a Target, where we bought the essentials since we didn't have anything—toothbrush, toothpaste, hairbrush, clean underwear, and extra clothes. "But let's get inside."

I nodded, grabbed my bag from the car's trunk, and followed her inside.

From the outside, the place looked like a one-story log cabin with a front porch with rocking chairs. On the inside, it followed the log theme with rustic furniture, thick rugs, heavy curtains, and wood accents.

Shade came inside carrying a few shopping bags from our Walmart stop.

I dropped my bag on the couch and went to help him. As we organized the groceries, Britta joined us and prepared pasta with Alfredo sauce. Though it was past ten, we hadn't had dinner yet.

After putting everything away, I set up the table and

Shade went to claim one of the three bedrooms. I would have one to myself, while Anna and Britta shared the third one.

"Dinner is ready!" Britta called out.

The table was for six and none of us took the ends. Shade sat by my side, while Anna and Britta sat across from us. We served ourselves and ate in silence.

We had been quiet most of the day, only speaking when necessary. But it wasn't just the silence, it was the tension that came with it. It was like a rubber band around us, stretched thin. There was so much to discuss, and yet, no one spoke a single word.

When everyone was done eating, Anna got up.

"Are we going to pretend nothing is happening?" I asked.

Anna sat down and looked at Britta, who of course, looked at her sister.

"Well," Britta started. "We all need some rest and clarity before we do anything."

"We spent the entire day in the car doing nothing more than thinking," I said. "I think we're all rested and have had enough time to think."

"I'm dead tired," Anna argued. "And my mind is still jumbled. Let's have a good night's sleep, and tomorrow after breakfast, we can talk."

Shade nodded. "I agree. I think I'll take a quick shower and go to sleep."

He had spent the entire day behind the wheel; I knew he was tired. I was too, I couldn't lie. What was it about spending the day in the car that made you so tired? But it was true. And yet, if it depended on me, I wouldn't relent so easily.

But it didn't depend on me.

I pushed to my feet. "I'm sure tomorrow you'll find some other excuse to postpone the conversation again." I grabbed my plate, utensils, and cup, and took them to the sink.

Then I marched to the front door.

"Hazel, where are you going?" Britta asked.

"To the porch," I said, my voice tight. "I want a few minutes of fresh air." Hopefully, it would help calm my mind.

"Just ..." Anna started, but I cut her a glare. She swallowed. "Just stay close to the cabin and don't take too long."

I rolled my eyes and walked out onto the porch. The chilly night air greeted me, and I braced myself, knowing that in about five minutes, I would regret leaving my jacket inside.

I sat on one of the rocking chairs, closed my eyes, and tried to enjoy the moment—the cold breeze, the fresh scent, the night sounds coming from the trees.

Mindful meditation. Mind over matter.

I opened my eyes and sighed. Yeah, right. I wished that worked for me.

Birds moved around the trees, and I frowned at the dark leaves in the distance. Did birds fly around at night? I thought they were quiet at this time.

The flapping of wings grew louder, and a small shape

emerged from one of the trees, flying down toward the cabin.

I shot to my feet, ready to retreat, but the bird was faster.

Only, it wasn't a bird.

I stretched my arms and the paper, folded like a bird, landed on my open palms. It stopped moving right away. Intrigued, I unfolded the paper.

Dear Hazel,

If you're reading this, then it means I'm dead.

No matter what you have heard, not all dark witches are evil. The Ashmist doesn't associate with the Darkmist and other evil covens, and we don't condone their evil acts. Some of us have good hearts and were born with dark gifts.

As were you, both in your previous life and this one.

Though, I'll argue you made a wrong decision in the previous one.

All we ask is for you to listen to us. Ultimately, what we would like is for you to see the mistakes of the past and correct it in the present for a better future for all of us.

Unfortunately, I can't help you understand that anymore, but you can talk to Starla, one of the lead witches in our coven, or even Guinevere, one of the instructors at the Light Castle—yes, she is one of us.

Just give my coven a chance.

A battle is coming, Hazel. It'll follow you even if you try to hide and you'll need all the help you can get. We can help you if you let us.

I know you'll do the right thing.

PS: when you're ready, all you need to do is write on the back of this note.

—Grace

I REREAD THE NOTE AT LEAST TWO MORE TIMES. STARLA WAS dead along with Grace, but Guinevere? Wow, I had no idea. The Lightgrove coven had no idea either.

Holding the note, I entered the cabin and found Anna and Britta at the kitchen, washing the dishes and cleaning up. They both stopped and looked at me.

"What is it?" Britta asked, her voice laced with worry.

"A note from Grace," I whispered, confused.

Anna dried her hands in the dishcloth and rushed to me. She grabbed the paper and smelled it. "She enchanted it, probably with a strand of your hair."

My brows shot to my hairline. "What?"

With a sigh, Anna read the note out loud. Britta's eyes rounded with each sentence. When she was done, Anna lowered the note and stared at Britta, a million words zipping between them.

"There." I pointed to Anna and then Britta. "I can see you're hiding something. Say it!"

"Hazel ..." Britta sighed.

I picked up the note from Anna. "Grace said I made the wrong decision in the past. Why?"

"You don't understand," Anna said.

"Of course, I don't. How can I understand something

no one explained to me. Tell me what it is. What did I do? Why—?"

I gasped as the world around me changed.

Inside what looked like a large room with several chairs in neat rows, I stood with Anna and Britta, and the other girl I had seen before.

Jewell.

"You don't understand," Jewell cried, her dark eyes full of tears.

"Then explain it to me," I said, my chest constricted.

"I shouldn't have to." She stood taller. "You're just like me. You should know."

I blinked and stared at Anna and Britta's weary faces in the cabin's living room.

"Who's Jewell?" I asked. The sisters inhaled deeply. "I've seen her before in a couple of memories, but only know I talked to her." I knew her name.

"Hazel, it's complicated," Britta said, her voice low.

She and Anna exchanged another look.

"Oh my God, you two!" I curled my hands into fists. "Why can't you just use your words and talk to me."

"Hazel ..." Anna reached for me.

I took a step back. "You know what? Now *I* don't want to talk to you." I picked up my bag from the couch and headed to the back, where the bedrooms were. "Good night," I snapped.

The hallway was short and had four doors. One was closed, which meant Shade was in there. Another one was the bathroom. And the other two were the remaining bedrooms. After a quick glance inside, I found the one with just one bed.

I stepped in and slammed the door shut.

It shook with the force and rattled my head.

Childish? Yes, but right now, I couldn't care less.

THIS TIME, I REALLY DIDN'T SLEEP WELL, IF AT ALL. I TOSSED and turned all night, too wound up with my argument with the sisters, and also with all the problems surrounding us.

Especially Sean.

He filled every corner and spare inch of my brain, and I wanted to scream every time I remembered his last half grin.

"We'll meet again, my love."

I shuddered. I wanted to see him. Right now. Yesterday. Tomorrow. Forever. But first, I needed to reverse what Queen Catarina had done to him.

But how?

At five in the morning, I was tired of fighting with my bed. I pushed the covers aside, brushed my hair, put on leggings and a sweater, and tiptoed out of the room. After a quick stop in the bathroom to wash my face and brush my teeth, I walked into the living/dining/kitchen area of the cabin, and found Anna and Britta seated around the dining table holding mugs with steam floating up.

They both looked at me and I froze.

"Morning," I grumbled, heading for the kitchen.

"There's hot water in the kettle," Britta said.

"And muffins in the oven," Anna added. "They will be ready in five minutes."

I grabbed a mug from the cabinet, a chamomile tea bag from the counter, and sat down across from them, my eyes on the window behind them. The curtains were drawn, and since it was still dark out, all I could see was a reflection of the interior.

Frowning, I took a sip of my tea. Weren't we in hiding? Was it safe to have the curtains open like that? What if the Brotherhood or Queen Catarina's witches were closing in on us? They could see us from outside, but we wouldn't see them.

I shook my head and dismissed those thoughts. It was too early to worry about anything.

"Hazel, we need to talk," Anna started.

And there went my no-worrying moment.

I took another sip from my tea.

"We think it's time to make a plan," Britta said.

I sucked in a breath. Of course, they wanted to talk about a plan, not about whatever they were hiding from me. It didn't matter. Soon, hopefully, I would have all my memories back, or at least most of them, and I would remember it all myself.

"I bet you already have a plan in mind." I drank some more of my tea.

"Yes, we—" The oven dinged. Anna shut her mouth and got up. She took the muffin pan from the oven, put it on the range, grabbed three plates, put a muffin on each, and brought them to the table. She sat down and passed one of the plates to me.

"Thank you." The cinnamon scent hit my nose, and I almost forgave both of them right there and then. I cleared my throat. "You were saying?" I bit down on my muffin.

And suddenly, I was someplace else.

My mother, wearing simple clothes and a thick apron, cut a piece of cake from the heavy pan on the table, put it on a plate, and offered it to me. I grabbed the plate, but I passed it to Anna, who was seated beside me. The next one, I handed to Britta, the next one to Jewell, the following one to my sister, Aurelia, and the last one was mine.

We all smiled at each other, inhaled the cinnamon goodness, and then dug in.

"Girls!" my mother berated through laughter. "You'll all choke like that!"

But we didn't care. We just wanted to devour this amazing thing that my mother cooked.

"Hazel?"

I shook my head and stared at Anna and Britta, who watched me closely.

"What did you see?" Britta asked. Shit. They already knew when I zonked out and had a memory.

I shrugged. "Just us as teenagers at my house, eating my mother's cinnamon cake."

Britta and Anna smiled.

"Oh, those were so good," Anna said with a sigh.

Britta nodded. "They were."

I remembered loving them, but I didn't exactly remember their taste. I picked up the half-eaten muffin. "I bet these are just as good."

Anna frowned. "I think we miss those so much, because of what they meant to us."

I knew what she meant. Back then, it was rare to eat such things. At that time, I hadn't cared about coven politics or leading my own coven. I hadn't met Prince Thales yet; he hadn't helped me in my endeavors. We hadn't fought the Brotherhood, other witches, or started a revolution.

Back then, we were poor, carefree, but happy.

I stilled. Whoa, that was more than I remembered a moment ago—not exactly images, but feelings and certainty.

"Anyway," I said, clearing my throat again. "We should talk about the plan."

"We know there's a problem inside the Light Castle," Britta said. "There seems to be at least one group of dark witches who don't associate with the Darkmist, the Darkmist witches themselves, and the Brotherhood. We need to deal with them all."

"And Sean," I added. That was on the top of my list. "We need to save him."

"Right," Anna said. "But we can't face them all right now. Not until you're at your full strength and have recovered all of your memories."

My brows curled down. "But that could take months, even if you help me with training."

"True." Britta nodded. "That's why we think we should find your necklace, your grimoire, and your ashes. The moment we find those, your power should return."

"All at once," Anna continued. "And your memories too."

"But ... do we know where those items are?" I asked.

"Not really." Britta leaned back on the chair, looking defeated. "We know where we last saw them."

"After you died, we took care of your things," Anna said. "Prince Thales hid them in the castle. When things started to go awry, when the dark witches and the Brotherhood became too much for us to fight, and we had to flee, we left your things, knowing they would be safe."

"We took the grimoire, though," Britta said.

"Oh, yeah, we did." Anna nodded. "We needed it for some spells."

"But years later, when we came back for them, they were gone," Britta said. "And we lost the grimoire during a bloody battle with the Brotherhood."

I inhaled sharply. "The Brotherhood has the grimoire?"

"We don't think so," Anna said. "Or at least, if a European sector of the Brotherhood got it back then, it didn't share it with the rest of the world."

I drank the last of my tea, now cold and too sweet. "Hm, so we need the items. That's a wish list, not a plan."

"Well ..." Britta got up and grabbed a notepad and pen from one of the kitchen's drawers, then sat back in her chair. "We can make a list of where we took each item, and where we have last seen them." She started scribbling on the notepad but not with words, with runes.

Arianna's runes.

My runes.

I frowned. "What are you writing?"

She stopped and glanced at the paper. "Hm, it's our secret code, remember? I'm just writing—"

"Places the items could be," I read, even though the notepad was upside down to me.

Her lips stretched into a smile. "You remember."

"Not only that." I took the notepad and pen from her and started drawing runes. Not my runes, but ... "These were the runes carved on the floor each time the lightning struck." Beside them, I wrote the original rune, with slight differences. I pushed the notepad closer to them. "See?"

Anna and Britta leaned over the notepad and their eyes went wide.

"These look like clues," Anna whispered. She grabbed the pen from me. "Here. This rune indicates the necklace, right?" She drew a straight line with a small circle at one end, and a third circle around it. "But look at this one." She traced the new rune I had drawn. "This is an arrow instead of the pendant at the edge. Where was this? What was it pointing to?"

I closed my eyes, trying to remember. I had been in the Light Castle's ballroom at that moment. "Hm, it pointed to the painting of the castle in Grandisia."

"By the light, these are all clues," Britta said. She pointed to the next one. "And this one?"

"This one hit when I was in the French Quarter," I told them. All of the runes had arrows, and in their matching original versions, they didn't. "It was pointing toward me."

I focused on details. "I was holding my grimoire, where I'm supposed to write down everything I learned during the initiate program."

"And the third?" Britta asked.

"I was in the Light Castle's throne room."

Anna stared at the notepad before making some notes. "So ... The necklace is at the castle in Grandisia, the grimoire is at the house in Venopolis, and the ashes are at the Light Castle?"

"What house in Venopolis? You mean, in Italy?" I asked, confused.

"What do you think?" Anna looked at Britta, ignoring me.

Britta nodded. "Sounds about right."

I shook my head. "It seems too good to be true." And too easy. Why hadn't anyone found this out yet?

"But it's the only clue we have, and it seems plausible." Britta stood from the chair again. "We gotta try."

I stared at her. "So ... we're going to Europe?"

She nodded. "Yes, we are. Pack your bags."

4

___

IT WASN'T LIKE I HAD A LOT TO PACK. AND EVEN THOUGH WE wanted to rush, there were a lot of problems we had to solve first: buying airplane tickets, which required money and passports. The money was no problem. Apparently, Anna, Britta, and Shade had inherited a lot of Prince Thales's fortune and had been keeping good investments since then.

As for the passport, I didn't have one. Never had the need for one. So, Anna contacted someone she had worked with before, who made false documents and paperwork. That would take two days. And then there was the flight—we were able to book four tickets to Grandisia for three days out.

In the meantime, the sisters trained me to sharpen my magic and hopefully get more of my powers and memories back. Shade acted like our errand boy—he went shopping for more clothes, thicker jackets, suitcases, and food to keep us here for another handful of days.

The training unlocked my magic and memories. I could control a fraction more of lightning now, and I had had three more memories about working on spells with Anna, Britta, and the mysterious Jewell, and of when I introduced Shade to my mother and Aurelia, who had been ecstatic about me getting a familiar.

Then it was finally time to go. Thankfully, the sisters were powerful, and they enchanted my fake passport so no one would ever detect it wasn't the real thing—like theirs.

"We have been doing this forever," Anna told me as we passed through the airport's security. We had decided to take a flight out of Jackson, Mississippi, instead of New Orleans, in case anyone decided to look for us there. "It's a necessity when you're immortal."

From Jackson, we flew to New York, then we took an overnight flight to Germany. There, we rented a car and drove southwest, where Grandisia once was.

Grandisia had been a small but rich country. After a long, bloody war about five hundred years ago, it had been abolished and its lands were absorbed by France and the German states.

Despite its demise, the former village turned capital, Fovere, had become a tourist point, and its most famous attraction was the palace.

It was the middle of the afternoon when Shade took an exit and merged onto a smaller road. "We're almost there," he said.

There were lots of cars coming and going. After a wide bend in the road, the town came into view. I gasped as a sense of longing hit me. I couldn't exactly see the village as it once was in my head, but I knew the hotels and restaurants and shops were new. Something about it instantly called to me.

This was where Arianna had met Prince Thales. This was where she had founded the Lightgrove coven. This was where she had died.

Where I had died.

My heart squeezed.

Shade rolled onto Main Street and I took everything in —the streets were paved, but the side roads were narrow and made of cobblestone. There were wide sidewalks, tall streetlamps, and tourists. A lot of tourists.

Shade turned another corner. "There it is."

I looked ahead and my breath caught.

The castle.

It looked tall and proud perched on a hill at the end of the road, a typical medieval castle with big gray stones, large gaps for windows, and turrets on the corners.

It wasn't the prettiest castle, but the more I stared at it, the more connected I felt to the past.

"Any memories?" Anna asked, eyeing me.

I shook my head. "Just ... feelings. Nostalgia. A sense of belonging."

She nodded. "This was home."

"It still is," Britta said, wistful.

Shade turned again and the castle disappeared behind the buildings. My chest constricted at not being able to see it. I didn't know if that was amusing or stupid. Or just part of a life with magic.

I let out a long sigh and reminded myself that we

would visit the castle tomorrow. The sisters had told me that booking was months in advance, but we would magic our way in again.

Shade entered the curved driveaway of a hotel and parked the car in front of the sliding glass doors. "Off we go," he said.

We hopped out of the car—jeez, it was cold here—as a bellman and a valet approached us. Shade handed the car keys to the valet, while the bellman helped us with our bags.

We checked in and were escorted to our adjoining rooms. After being on the go for almost twenty-four hours, I was tired but at the same time, energized.

"Can we go exploring?" I asked the sisters. Shade had already disappeared into the bathroom for a shower.

"We'll definitely go out for dinner," Anna said with a frown. "But I'm not sure we should go out in public yet."

"We don't know if there are Brotherhood members in town," Britta explained. "Last thing we want is to warn them of our presence before we are able to accomplish our mission."

I nodded. "I get it." But that made me sad. This had been our hometown. Where we all lived, where we all grew up.

Anna patted my shoulder. "I know you want to see everything with your own eyes, but truth is, little remains of our home."

"You'll at least see the castle tomorrow," Britta said with a smile.

"True," I conceded.

"Let's take a shower, go out for a bite, and then rest. It has been a long day," Anna said.

Britta clicked her tongue. "Long two days."

"Right." Anna waved at me from the door that connected our rooms, then disappeared into the bathroom.

I unpacked my change of clothes and toiletries, and waited until Shade was done with his shower. Ten minutes later, he emerged with damp hair, and wearing slacks and a sweater.

I tilted my head. "Do you always dress this fancy?"

He stared at me. "I was a cat for the first part of my life. The moment Anna and Britta made me a human, I decided I wouldn't be an ordinary one."

A cat shifter human still attached to a dead witch. My brows curled down. "Do you still feel it? The familiar connection?"

There had been a couple of moments where I had felt it, but I couldn't explain it.

He stared at me and nodded. "I haven't felt it since the day you died." His voice was somber. "But it started again when you were born. A faint feeling deep in here." He pressed his hand to his chest. "Since we've visited the Wildthorn witches, it has increased. Slowly, but it has."

It was probably strange for him to be here with me, to know there was this huge connection between us, and still, feel like strangers.

"We'll figure this—"

Suddenly, I was ten years old. It was late at night, and I had been crying. This was the day my powers had first shown, and my mother had yelled at me for ruining our lives. She was inside the house with my sister, packing our things so we could leave before the town came for us and turned us in to the Brotherhood.

With a sulk, I sat on the rough stones that served as steps to our tiny house's back door and looked up at the moon. Such a beautiful night, with a bright full moon illuminating the back-yard, which really, it was green grass that stretched to the forest beyond. The houses in the village were either smushed together, or spread apart in the field.

I inhaled deeply, trying to take in the beauty of the moon and pushing my bad mood away.

A tug inside my chest made me gasp. I looked at the lawn and saw a black cat a few feet from me.

"Hi, there." I looked side to side. "Where did you come from?"

The cat meowed and approached me. I tentatively reached my hand to touch him, but the cat jumped in my lap and rubbed his side against my stomach.

An energy filled me, and the tug came back.

I knew it then. "You're my familiar," I whispered in awe. None of the witches I knew had a familiar. They were consid-ered too weak to have one. But this shiny black cat was all mine. I petted the cat's head, and it purred in pleasure. "Aren't you pretty? I should give you a name." The moon shone bright, but he had approached me without me seeing, as if he blended well with the darkness. "How about Shade?" The cat let out a short meow that sounded like a yes to me and I smiled. "Nice to meet you, Shade. I promise to take care of you."

"Hazel?"

I opened my eyes and stared at Shade, who watched me with a frown. "I ... I just saw when you first came to me."

He nodded. "I remember that night. Not even a few hours after I found you, we moved to another town." He gestured to the window behind me. "This town, actually."

That same tug pressed against my chest and sadness washed over me. "I said I would take care of you. Then I died and left you alone."

He pressed his lips into a thin line. "I fell into a depression after that. If it weren't for Britta, Anna, and Thales, I think I wouldn't have lasted another week without you."

"I'm sorry," I whispered.

He waved me off, cleared his throat, and walked past me, toward one of the beds. "The past is in the past." He kept his back to me, as if he didn't want me to see how much all of this affected him. I couldn't say I blamed him.

So, I grabbed my clothes and walked into the bathroom.

5

EARLY THE NEXT MORNING, WE HAD BREAKFAST IN THE hotel, and then set off toward the castle. I kept getting distracted by the mix of old and new as we walked the narrow stone streets. We passed through shops with merchandise about the castle, the royal family, the town, the witch hunts, and even mini spell books said to contain the secret spells used by the witches who had lived here. I wanted to see it all, but Anna and Britta wouldn't let me.

Just like last night, when we ventured out of the hotel and went to the bistro across the street for dinner and then back to our rooms.

However, last night, when crossing the street to go back to the hotel, we saw a group of Brotherhood of Purity members a block down, strolling down the street as if they were part of the tourist attraction. When I first saw them, I panicked, then I saw people asking to take pictures with them and relaxed slightly.

"Don't let that fool you," Britta said. "They are authentic. They put up with the tourists to blend in."

As we hurried away, the sisters explained that the Brotherhood still had a heavy presence in every village, town, and city in Europe, so sure they were that witches were hiding in every corner.

That night, I dreamed a Brotherhood member invaded our hotel room and attacked me.

Now in the daylight, it was easier to be brave and pretend the Brotherhood wasn't around. Although, we all kept watch for them.

When we reached the road that led to the castle, all the distraction faded away. I gawked at the looming structure on the hill, the sun rising behind it, casting golden light across its walls. I squinted, trying to remember. I must have come this way so many times in my previous life; it was impossible not to have any memories of it.

But none came to me.

We joined the procession of tourists and walked toward the castle's gates. Most people veered toward the guest services counter to the right to purchase tickets even though several signs said it was sold out for the next three months.

"Tickets, please," an older man dressed in royal blue army attire said.

"Here." Anna handed him four blank papers she had cut from a notepad she had found in our hotel room.

The man stared at the paper for a moment, then bowed his head and gestured past the gates. "Follow the path to the right. You'll meet the guide. Enjoy your visit."

"Thank you," she said.

We walked past the man, my heart pounding. I knew he wouldn't realize the tickets were fake. Anna was powerful, and her spell would hold for days, or even years, if she willed it, but I couldn't help the mix of exhilaration and fear that swam inside my veins.

We followed the crowd down the path found a handful of people dressed in the same royal blue uniform dividing the tourists in smaller groups.

"This one," Britta said, guiding us toward the woman to the left, who was nearest the castle's front garden.

I followed them, but my eyes kept darting side to side, taking everything in. I could see the old construction mixed with the new—the ticket booth, the entrance, the restrooms, and gift shop—but none of it took away from the beauty of this place.

Had I thought this castle wasn't attractive from a distance? Maybe that was because I had seen too many Disney movies and imagined royal castles all looked like Cinderella's. But this place was different. It was stronger, sturdier, and powerful.

"Welcome to Griss Castle," the woman said. Her dark hair was pulled back in a severe ponytail, and she reminded me of a mean general. "My name is Patricia, and I'll be your guide this morning. We'll start the tour inside the castle." She gestured to the stone steps behind her and the giant double doors beyond them. "Please, don't touch anything and remain with the group. There are several restricted areas in the castle. You'll see those are cordoned off with obvious signs." She smiled at us. "Shall we begin?"

She started for the stairs and our group followed her.

I took three steps and then turned to look at the expansive garden to the right.

A blue carriage with beautiful white horses pulled up to the steps. Soldiers in dark blue uniform patrolled the gates. Beyond the gates, the stone road stretched out to the old village—my home—in the distance.

"Arianna?"

I snapped to attention and turned. Prince Thales stood atop the stairs, his hand stretched to me, and a wide smile on his lips.

My heart skipped a beat. It still shocked me how much Thales was the perfect likeness to Sean—maybe because I had seen only old paintings of him. But now that I knew who he was, it all made sense.

"Are you nervous?" he asked, his smile losing its shine for a moment.

I inhaled, still stunned. He looked so handsome in his blue uniform and all the medals hanging from his chest. He was a decorated soldier, a leader to his people, the crown prince, and a trusted advisor to his father. He was kind to his mother and a good brother to his little sister.

Why was I hesitating? I stretched my hand to his ...

And then I was shaken and found myself back in the present.

"A memory?" Shade whispered.

The group was moving inside the castle, and Anna and Britta were a few steps in front of us.

I nodded. "I have a feeling I'll have many of them inside."

"It would make sense." He tugged at my sleeve. "Let's go."

I followed him, though I was still dazed from the whiplash the memories gave me.

Two guides, dressed in that same uniform, stood by the open doors and greeted us as we walked in. I held my breath as I stepped into the immense castle's foyer—it was so large, it looked like a ballroom. The rough gray stone from the outside was replaced by smooth off-white stones for the floor. Several wide archways lined the sides, and between them, tapestries of the countryside covered the walls.

A woman dressed in the finest gown I had ever seen walked under one of the archways, followed by a handmaid and a castle guard.

"You must be Arianna," she said.

In the far back, a wide staircase led to the second floor and opened to a large landing that led left and right.

A little girl stood atop the landing, dressed in a white night-gown, and waved at me when I walked in, a huge smile on her lips.

Over the landing, three paintings that were now faded with time covered the entire wall, depicted three different royal families, and right in the middle was King Norbert and Queen Hella seated on their thrones, with Prince Thales and Princess Louise standing by their side. A thick blue rope cut in front of the paintings, keeping tourists away.

"This looks recent," I said, examining the painting.

Prince Thales nodded. "My father commissioned it a few months ago, when my sister started getting sick."

"This way, please," our guide said, calling our group past one of the archways.

I grabbed Shade's arm, suddenly dizzy. "I'm having too many memories."

"That's good, though," he said.

It was, but if I kept having memories every two seconds, then I would faint.

We walked down a wide hallway and stopped in front of another set of larger-than-life doors.

The guide gestured to the doors. "This is the library." A thick blue cord made an arc a few feet inside the library. We could step in, take a peek, but we couldn't go any farther.

I waited my turn, then walked into the viewing area. The library had an open space right at its entrance. Just beyond it was a long wooden table with several chairs. Every couple of feet, metal candle holders jutted up from the table.

I sat at the middle of the table, hunched over a thick book, and piles of books spread over the table around me.

The candle flickered and I cursed under my breath. "There has to be a draft in here," I said, looking around the otherwise dark library. I glanced at the tall shelves filled with thousands of books, but I could barely see anything at this time of the night.

"Yes?" the guide asked.

A young woman lowered her hand. "Is it true Prince Thales fell in love with a witch?"

I stilled. Shade looked at me. Anna's and Britta's eyes widened.

The guide smiled. "That is one of the most famous stories from that era. Prince Thales did indeed fall in love with a young woman from the village, and she was persecuted during the witch hunts, but I'm afraid, witches don't exist."

"And killed?" the young woman asked.

"We think so," the guide answered. "Recordings and knowledge from King Norbert's era are few and mysterious. Perhaps they were hiding witches in their midst." She winked, and then moved down the hallway to another archway. "This is the Inviso gallery."

We stopped in front of the archway, and just like the library, a rope created a fence inside the room. We could step in a few feet, take a peek at the various paintings and busts filling the room, but that was it.

"Here you'll see portraits and busts of the royal families, along with other illustrious people from that time." She pointed to a bust to the left. "This one, for example, was of a decorated soldier from a thousand years ago. Stories go that he single-handedly defeated a group from a nearby German state sent to infiltrate the country."

"So, the German states were already interested in these lands?" a man asked.

The guide nodded. "Germany and France. There are records of battles between the German states and France from Grandisia's founding until its final breath five hundred years ago."

"It was witches," the same young woman from before said.

The guide pressed her lips into a thin line. "The witch hunts were real, and there were rumors of powerful covens in the region, but once again, witches don't exist. They didn't exist then either. Women who were thought to be witches might have contributed to the fall of Grandisia, but they certainly weren't the main reason." She gestured down the hall. "Let's keep moving."

"Get ready," Anna whispered.

We remained at the back of the group, walking slowly. The guide turned down a long hallway that led to the throne room—how did I know that?—but we didn't. Once they were out of sight, we moved.

Anna walked to the wall and placed a hand underneath one of the metal sconces that dotted the surface every ten feet. She pushed, and a portion of the wall moved, revealing a secret door.

"The servants' corridor," I said, remembering it.

Anna smiled at me. "You're remembering."

"More than I thought I would." But still nothing that would lead me to the missing necklace.

"That's good," Britta said as she walked through the small door. We all followed suit.

Anna closed the door behind us, and we were engulfed by darkness. She brought her hand up and a ball of white light illuminated our surroundings.

The hallway was wide and tall enough for a person of average height to walk through without bumping into the rough walls and ceiling. The floor was rough and uneven. The sconces were crude and covered in cobwebs.

"These service corridors weren't a secret," Britta said. "We should assume the humans managing the castle know about them, so be careful."

"There are other, secret passageways," I whispered.

"Do you remember them?" Anna asked, sounding eager.

I frowned, thinking. "Not really. I remember knowing about them. I know I have used many of them before, but I can't remember where."

"It's okay," Britta said. "We'll use what we know."

We started walking down the corridor, and when we came to a fork, we separated. I created a light like Anna's and turned to the left, with Shade coming with me, while Anna and Britta went to the right.

The plan was to search for the necklace in rooms where the public wasn't allowed. Prince Thales's chambers, the guest room I used whenever I stayed in the castle, maybe even Thales's study since he had spent a lot of time there.

The sisters were hoping I would be able to sense the necklace once I was in the castle, but so far I hadn't felt a thing.

"I came often to the castle, didn't I?" I asked.

"You did."

"Did you come with me?"

"Most of the time." Shade tsked. "In the beginning, I didn't like Thales."

I glanced at Shade from over my shoulder. "What? Did I know that?"

Shade huffed. "Everyone knew. I would try to scratch him." He let out a soft chuckle.

"Why?"

"I thought ... he was going to take you away from me."

My heart squeezed and I stopped. "Oh, Shade."

He raised a finger. "I know a connection between a witch and a familiar is special, different from a romantic one, but deeper in some way. Don't worry, I had never had those kinds of thoughts about you, but still, I knew Thales would replace me."

"What made you change your mind?"

"You," he said simply. "You made a point of showing me you cared about me, and that even if we allowed Thales into our lives, you would always care for me."

Our lives. Because a witch and her familiar were always together.

I held his hand. "I'm glad."

He squeezed my hand. "And Thales was nice to me. He tried bribing me with treats, so ..." He shrugged.

I smiled.

Shade let go of my hand and cleared his throat. "We should be arriving in the south wing soon."

I took the hint and turned, resuming our walk through the corridor. I was a little disappointed about not having memories of Shade scratching Thales, or Thales bribing Shade, but I knew they would come.

We were making progress each day.

And soon, I would have the necklace and be one step

closer to getting my full powers ... and saving Sean. My chest constricted every time I remembered he was somewhere out there, living his days as a dark, evil demon.

I had to undo that sooner rather than later.

We marched on until, finally, we reached the end of the corridor. I flicked the light upward so it floated on its own, and pressed my hand against the wall, finding the almost imperceptible seam in the door. I pushed the door open, light spilling inside the corridor. My floating light faded like smoke.

I stepped aside and beckoned toward the door. "Please."

With a half smile, Shade bowed his head and stepped through the door.

I took a step to follow him—

A hand closed around my wrist and yanked me back. I yelped and the door closed.

"Hazel!" I heard Shade's muffled shout. "What happened? I can't open it!"

With trembling hands, I created another white light.

And came face-to-face with Sean.

He tilted his head, a lopsided grin on his lips. "I said we would meet again, my love."

6

I couldn't believe my eyes. I was dreaming. No …

Sean's pallor was freakishly white, dark veins adorned his black eyes, and he had a wolfish smile.

Not a dream, a nightmare, then.

I took a step back, pressing into the corridor's wall. "W-what are you doing here?"

He didn't answer me. Instead, he glanced at the unmarked door, where Shade was still punching and yelling for me. With a growl, Sean grabbed my wrist and pulled me away from the door.

"Hey!" I dug in my heels, I pulled my weight back, I tried holding on to the sconces on the walls, but all that did was hurt my hands. Sean had always been a lot stronger than me, and now as a demon, he was unnaturally strong. "Let me go!"

He stopped and I fell into him. He loomed over me, his eyes menacing. "Stop irritating me, or this will get deadly in the blink of an eye."

I inhaled deeply. This was certainly not Sean, not my Sean anyway.

He surged forward, taking me with him through the dark corridor. My light floated behind us, barely illuminating the way. I could use magic, hurt him, and flee, but I didn't really want to hurt him. I could create a barrier when he let go of me and run. And then what? Would I be able to find the necklace and escape before he caught up with me again?

Unlikely.

I frowned as we continued down the corridor and an idea struck me. I started reaching for my phone. Maybe I could text Shade and the sisters, let them know—

"Drop the phone before I break it," he warned, danger in every syllable.

I let the phone go, for now. "How did you find me?"

"Apparently, this new me comes with some pretty cool powers." He turned to me and walked backward as he raised his hand and shadows twirled around us like dancing serpents.

My eyebrows shot up in surprise.

"That's not all." He whirled his back to me and flicked his finger.

My light poofed from existence. In complete darkness, I stopped walking, but he didn't. He pulled me along with him.

"I can see in the dark," he said. "But that's not even the best part."

He didn't continue and I knew he wanted me to play a part in this charade.

After a few more steps, he finally stopped. He pushed one of the secret doors open and faint light streamed through the small crack.

I sighed. "What is the best part?"

A line of light cut through his devilish face, and he grinned at me, that evil half grin of his. "I can sense you."

My eyes bugged. "What?"

He nodded. "It's faint. I have to use all of my power to snatch it, but it's there." He leaned closer and I felt the will to move the opposite way. "I knew you hid in a cabin for several days two hours north of New Orleans, as I knew when you were headed to the airport. So, I followed you."

"And what exactly is your plan?" I asked, my voice trembling. "Kill me? Capture me and hand me over to Catarina?"

His eyes narrowed. "Catarina sent me once she realized what I could do, but I'll let you in on another secret: I don't trust her."

"Aren't you her demon? Her pet?" I knew that was a low jab, but I needed to see his reaction.

His eyes flared with rage. "I am not hers. She might have changed me, but I owe her nothing. I'm here because I wanted to find you for myself."

A sudden lump lodged in my throat, and I forced myself to swallow it. "Why?"

Slowly, he lifted his hand and tucked a loose strand of my blond hair behind my ear. His fingers lingered on my neck, and if it weren't for his oddly cold touch, I would have melted.

By all that was holy, this was torture.

"Because you belong with me, and I belong with you." His voice was low, as if saying it out loud was sin. "Seven hundred years ago, we belonged to each other, heart, body, and soul."

I shook my head. "I belonged to the previous you. Not to this tainted version."

His eyes sparked with fury. "That version was weak and blinded by love. I'm stronger, more focused, more fun. You'll learn to love me like this." He leaned into me, brushing his lips on my ear, and I fought a mix of fearful shudder and lusty shiver. "If you won't, then I'll make you like me."

"Sean," I whispered, a silent plea hidden in that single word.

He straightened then. "We don't have time to waste." Still holding my wrist, he pushed the door open and stepped through, pulling me with him.

The bright light coming from the windows blinded me, and I lifted one hand to shield it. When my sight adjusted, I looked around, confused.

We were in a hallway. One side was a solid wall with tapestries and fancy decorations, the other was lined with narrow windows that overlooked the garden beyond the castle.

I glanced at the now closed door, almost invisible within the wall again. "I don't remember this one."

"But I do," Sean said, his eyes darting around, as if expecting someone to march into this hallway at any moment.

"Wait." I stared at him. "You're having memories?"

He lowered his gaze to meet mine. "A few."

How was that possible? The ritual Anna, Britta, and Queen Yira had done had been for me, not him. I thought he would remember as I did, or at least, once I had my full memories and my full power and could somehow spell them back to him.

"Since when?"

"Since Catarina freed me," he said. "At first, it was one or two. But since I arrived here, especially inside this place ... it has been more." He glanced around again, serious. "Even now, looking at these walls and windows. Sometimes I can't remember exact images, but I remember certain details, certain feelings."

Just like me. And if he was remembering his past life, as Prince Thales, then it meant that version of himself was still inside him. Leaping on this fragile hope, I took a step closer to him and placed my hand on his chest, right above his heart. He faced me, his brows knitted.

"Do you remember me? Us?" I asked, my voice low. "Arianna and Thales sneaking around the castle, two star-crossed lovers?" I rose on my tiptoes and stretched my neck. Probably unconsciously, he angled his head toward mine. "Do you remember being Thales?" An honorable, pure-hearted man who would never, ever become a demon.

I grazed my lips on his chin, and Sean sucked in a sharp breath. He brought his hand up, clasped around my nape, and brushed his lips over mine. I shivered and bit back on a moan ... by the light, I still desired him, I still loved him, and when he pressed his lips to mine and dove into an urgent kiss, I had trouble remembering why I had resisted him in the first place.

Three seconds later, Sean's hand shifted from my neck to my hair. He broke the kiss and tugged my hair down, tilting my head up painfully. "What games are you playing?" he asked through gritted teeth. "Your charms won't work like they use to, not until you become like me."

I froze. "What do you mean?"

"Just …" He groaned, released my hair, but took my wrist instead. "Just come with me."

We followed the hallway and three turns later, we arrived at a large study.

I blinked and suddenly there he was, standing behind the big mahogany desk, his eyes on the unrolled paper spread over it. He wore his dark blue uniform, but the top buttons were undone, and his hair was disheveled, probably from running his fingers over it so many times.

"What's the matter?" I asked.

He glanced up, startled. "God, I didn't even hear you enter."

A tug brought me back to the present.

"No time for more memories," Sean said.

"Did you see that too?"

He lowered his chin once as he moved across the room with purpose. Behind the desk, he released my hand, and for a moment, I wrestled again with what I should do. Blast him and run? Yell for Anna, Britta, and Shade? This was Prince Thales's study. They were bound to come this way. Shade knew something had happened. We had been separated and he couldn't open the door—probably Sean's doing. I was sure Shade had gone after Anna and Britta, which meant they were now looking for me, not the necklace.

All I had to do was stall. Once the sisters and Shade found me, they could help me stun Sean without hurting him, so we could find the necklace.

Leave Sean behind.

A pang cut through my heart.

"Here." Sean pushed the heavy carved wooden chair aside and knelt behind the desk. He opened a fake side panel from the desk's side, revealing a small trap door.

I frowned at him, not remembering it. Had I known about this one before?

The door unfolded, bigger than I first thought. It led to a steep and narrow staircase.

Sean gestured to the opening on the floor. "In you go."

Of course.

"A-are you sure? I'm claustrophobic."

"No, you're not in any of your lives." His eyes hardened. "Good try, though. Now go before I make you."

"But—"

"Hazel, I know what you're doing. Just go."

Shit. So much for stalling.

I conjured a small bolt of light to float above my shoulder, sat down on the floor, and scooted down the stairs. They were dusty and slippery, and as soon as I was fully inside the tunnels, a musty and moldy scent hit my nostrils. These secret passageways probably hadn't been used in at least five centuries, and I was certain we would find dead mice and whatnot down here.

The stairs went on for a long time, probably more than

an entire floor, until finally I reached the bottom. With magic, I made my light bolt brighter. The corridor here was a little wider and taller than the service ones, but it was still dark and creepy.

Sean's boots thumped on the rough stone after he jumped the last five steps.

He took the lead, as if he really remembered these tunnels. Maybe he did. He had confessed to having more memories, and I bet most of them were different from mine.

Still undecided about what to do, I followed him into the darkness.

7

———

Surprising me, Sean asked, "What item do you think is hidden in the castle?"

"I don't know."

He scoffed. "You're not a good liar, Hazel. The necklace, isn't it?" I tripped on my own feet and halted. Sean turned and narrowed his eyes at me. "It is the necklace." He took two steps closer to me. "Why do you think it's that?"

I shook my head.

And then I found myself somewhere else.

I stood in a small clearing in the forest behind the castle, with Thales in front of me, looking at me with his beautiful eyes. The crescent moon shone above our heads, illuminating enough of this place, this little corner of the world. My heart full, I glanced around.

A stone path zigzagged through the clearing, colorful flowers flanked the path, and every few feet, a tall torch flickered with the gentle night breeze.

In the center of the clearing, beside us, was a small pergola adorned by creepers and small pink flowers. A stone bench and a round fire pit sat under the pergola. A big wooden tray spilling with so much food had been placed over a small folding table beside the bench.

This was our secret place, which he had made for me, so we could meet without anyone knowing. I had enchanted it, warded its border, so no one else could find it.

"I have something for you," Thales said, his eyes fixed on mine. He placed a blue velvet box in my hands. I gasped as he opened it and a beautiful necklace with a thick silver chain, and a diamond-shaped blue gem. "I commissioned it myself."

"It's beautiful," I whispered.

"It's also magical."

"What?"

A sly grin took over his lips. "I asked your friends help with that. They took it for a few days, went to a place of power, and put a little of their magic in it during a ritual. After, they traveled around the region, and asked every powerful witch they knew to put a little of their magic in it too."

My eyes widened. So that was why Anna, Britta, and Jewell had been out for the past week. They said they were going to visit friends, but they had actually been visiting the powerful witches in the nearby towns.

"That's ... incredible."

"Anna told me they even met a group of witches who used wands," he said, amused. "Wands! Never heard of that one before."

"Until a few months ago, you didn't believe in witches at all."

"Well, true." He picked up the necklace from the box. "May I?"

I took a step back. "Thales, I can't. This is too much."

"Nothing is too much for you. If I could, I would give you the world."

"I don't want the world."

"Then at least accept this."

How could I not when he looked at me with wounded puppy eyes? He had made this necklace for me; other witches had enchanted it with their magic for me.

With a sigh, I nodded and turned my back to him. I lifted my hair and Thales placed the necklace around my neck. A faint click sounded when he closed the clasp, but he didn't move. Instead, he ran his fingers from my neck to the front of my throat, and then his breath was on my skin, and his body pressed against my back. I gasped when his lips touched below my ear and a delicious shiver ran down my spine.

"That is why," Sean said, clearing his throat.

I snapped back and looked around. We were still in the dark passageway, and I was sure he had seen what I had seen.

"You gave me the necklace," I whispered in awe.

He nodded. "I remembered commissioning it when I visited my study. I also remembered that you put your magic inside the necklace, and together with everyone else's, that necklace was one of the most powerful magical items that ever existed. And I'm sure I know where it's hidden."

I knew it too.

"Sean," I said, trying to stall again. I couldn't let him get to the necklace.

Unless this necklace was as powerful as everyone said, and once I got hold of it, I could use it to restore him to his former self.

Could I do it? Would it work? What was the alternative?

"Don't Sean me," he said with a bite. He wrapped his fingers around my wrist and yanked me forward.

We continued in silence, the only sound was the stomp of our footsteps echoing through the passageway.

Finally, after a few turns, a ramp down, and some steps, we arrived at a small doorway. Sean let go of me and searched the wall to the right. He jerked the bricks until he found a loose one. He pulled it out and then he pulled the metal key for the doorway—a giant, old, and rusty thing.

He unlocked the door, but it hadn't been used in so long, he had to use all of his strength to yank it open. We found ourselves face-to-face with a thick wall of ivy.

"Of course," he groaned, clearly annoyed.

He grabbed at the ivy with his bare hands and pulled it until the vines snapped—it would take us forever to make it to the other side like that.

"Step aside," I said.

He stopped, glanced at me over his shoulder, hesitated, but relented.

I zapped the ivy with my lightning. The ivy fried instantly, a narrow hole appearing in the center, letting a pinpoint of light enter. The scent of burnt leaves filled air.

Eyebrows raised, Sean showed me one of his lopsided

grins. I didn't know what to think of it anymore—was it still charming, or was it creepy?

Sean trudged past the ivy. I followed and squinted under the sun. I put a hand over my eyes and glanced around. We were away from the castle, past the back wall, where there was at least a half a mile of tall grass, and in the distance, the forest.

"Let's go," Sean started toward the trees.

I glanced down to myself. I was wearing a jacket, but not a thick one to be out in this weather, and my combat boots, which were extremely comfortable for going to classes and traveling, certainly hadn't been made for hiking.

With a sigh, I crossed my arms and started walking with him.

It wasn't a specific memory, but I remembered why the castle stood so far from the forest. The king had told me about it long ago. Because it would be easy for enemy armies to hide among the trees and if the forest was near the castle, they could find a way to infiltrate the castle and no one would know until it was too late. This way, even if their enemies were hiding behind the trees, they would have to come out in the open to approach the castle, giving them time to prepare for the attack.

The grass was kept shorter—there had been a herd of sheep and goats around the castle, just so they would eat the grass!

Now, though, the lawn was uncared for and came up to my knees. Each step forward was a struggle, and I was sure that I would twist my ankle.

It took us longer to cross that half mile than expected, and by the time we reached the trees, I had a thin layer of sweat down my spine and my breathing was shallow. I leaned onto a thick tree trunk to catch my breath and checked my phone—there was no cell reception here, but I could see the time: It was already noon.

If I had known this was how my day would go, I would have eaten a bigger breakfast or brought some water. At least, now I felt a little warmer.

Sean stepped right in front of me, with a foot separating us. One corner of his lips tugged up. "If I had to guess, I would say you had been a princess in the past life."

I frowned. "Well, as far as I can tell, you did treat me like a princess."

"Not in the beginning."

I had always known that. Whenever we studied the Lightgrove history, we were told Prince Thales was against Arianna helping his kingdom and often he was rude to her in front of everyone. But as they worked together, his opinion of her changed.

The moment Sean said those words, they flooded my brain with such truth, I gasped. It was one thing to know about it, but it was another to feel it.

I stared into his eyes, trying to figure him out. There were moments when he didn't act or look at me like a demon, and I caught a glimpse of either my Sean or Prince Thales.

Which one was he right now?

I reached for him, tracing the decorative gray stitch of his dark sweater right above the middle of his chest. He stopped breathing, his eyes darkening. By the light, how I wanted to touch him for real, for him to touch me. How I was dying to kiss him, to feel his body against mine again, and—

Clearing his throat, Sean took a step back. "Let's keep moving. We still have a way to go."

We walked deeper into the woods for another thirty minutes. I had moments when I knew exactly where we were, but those were fleeting, and then I assumed we were lost. Or I would have, if Sean didn't seem so sure of the way we were going.

Sean stopped and pressed a finger to his lips. "Shhh."

I almost bumped into him as I skidded to a stop. I looked around, searching for whatever he had seen or heard. Was it an animal? I searched my mind but couldn't remember if there had been any dangerous animals living in this forest.

The sounds of a branch snapping and crunching leaves reached my ears, and I turned to it. Five women walked leisurely toward us.

"There you are," a woman with long indigo hair said. She had a wicked smile, and I knew she and the others were witches. "For a moment there, I thought you were trying to run away."

"I told you he wasn't," another woman said. "He wouldn't be stupid to trick Queen Catarina."

My brows curled down. So, these were Darkmist witches. "They came with you," I said in a faint voice. He had told me he could feel me, that he had been sent, but he had never said if he had come alone.

Shit.

"They did," he said, his voice grave. "Because I had no choice in the matter." He took a step closer to me, half of his body in front of mine. "But now I do."

Without a warning, Sean raised his hands and tendrils of darkness lifted from the ground, fast and vicious like snakes. They wrapped around the witches, immobilizing them. Three screamed, panicking, while the indigo-haired one and the other witch fought the darkness. The indigo-hair witch blasted the serpent with one hand, while sending bolts of dark magic toward us. Sean twisted, grabbed my upper arms, and hid us behind a tree. He pushed me against the trunk while pressing his body against mine.

"What's going on?" I asked, trembling for more than one reason.

Sean didn't answer. Instead, he spied from behind the tree. A dark bolt zipped past his head, and he cursed under his breath.

He lowered himself a bit, tried again, and threw another snake of shadow their way. A scream filled the air, and I stilled. What had that been?

"Four down, one to go," he whispered. Tricking the remaining witch, Sean spied at her from the other side of the tree.

And that was when I saw a sixth witch coming from the opposite direction. With a winning smile, she raised her hand, ready to strike Sean in the back.

I acted. I brought my hand up and let my lightning out, along with all my rage.

It struck the witch's chest. Her eyes went wide, her body shook hard, and a second later, she fell with a heavy thud.

Sean looked back, a puzzled knot between his brows. His eyes met mine for a brief second, then he launched himself from behind the tree and sent dozens of dark snakes toward the witch.

I didn't hear anything. No scream, no thud, nothing, but that was probably because my eyes were trained to where the other witch had been, to where I had struck her.

Holy shit, I had killed a witch.

Sean appeared in front of me and held my upper arms again. "Hazel." He shook me gently. "Snap out of it."

"I ..." I closed my mouth and opened it again. "I killed her." My voice was barely above a whisper.

He pressed his lips tight. "She would have killed me. You saved me."

I shifted my gaze to his. His eyes were still dark, the black lines adorning his pretty, pale face. I had killed a dark witch to save my Sean, not this fake version.

Tears burned behind my eyes. "I thought they were on your side."

He shook his head once. "I'm on my own side, on our side."

"What?"

Sean slid his hands down my arms and held my hands in his. "I can't deny I'm glad Queen Catarina freed me, but do you really think I would work with her? *For* her? I stayed with her and the Darkmist witches while I was searching for you."

"What are you talking about?"

"Think about it, Hazel. I'm Prince Thales, now with this incredible magic, and you're Queen Arianna, one of the most powerful witches who ever lived. We don't need the Darkmist witches or the Lightgrove coven. We can find your things and create our own coven. We can come back here, stop this tourist crap, and reclaim our castle." He waved his hand to the distance. "We can be queen and king, as it should have been from the start."

I stared at him, at a loss for words.

I had killed a person to save him, this cruel, power-hungry demon. Oh my God, what had I done?

I pushed away from him and took several steps back. Then I saw the other witches—all on the ground, looking like mummies with their skin gray, their eyes wide, and their mouths hanging open in an eternal scream.

My stomach turned.

Maybe this wasn't the best idea. Maybe going with Sean to the clearing and finding the necklace was the wrong thing. He was too powerful. What if I couldn't revert the darkness inside of him with just the necklace? I probably needed all three items for that.

Distraught, I turned my back to him and started walking away.

A cold, dark rope wrapped around me, holding my arms against my body, and my legs in place.

Sean jerked the darkness and pulled me back toward him. "Don't be stupid, Hazel."

I fought against the rope, but it was magical. Unless I wanted to fry him, I couldn't fight it. A sob rose to my throat, but I pushed it down. I wouldn't cry in front of this demon. "I'm not stupid. I think I'm good, and that I care for others, and the world, and I do not want to kill or fight or go to war or take over castles! I want my Sean back and I want this nightmare to be over!"

He groaned. "I won't waste my time explaining things to you." He gave me his back and started marching ahead.

The rope tugged and I had to follow.

We weren't far from the clearing, I knew that. If I was going to do something, come up with a plan, it was now or never. But whenever I tried thinking, focusing, I felt like I was swimming in syrup. I felt sluggish, my mind slow, and all I could think of was that I had killed a witch, and that this Sean was even worse than I first thought. More powerful.

I was way out of my depth.

8

WE WALKED PAST A LINE OF THIN TREES AND ARRIVED AT THE clearing. I halted, stunned, and took it all in for a second.

The stone path was barely visible under the overgrown grass. Wildflowers grew everywhere, but mostly around a stone bench and the fire pit. The pergola had some broken pieces, and the wood had seen better days.

Still, this place held such magic, such history, that even the air felt rich. Here, the chilly weather and the wintry wind were left behind.

"Where's the necklace?" Sean asked, tugging on the rope again and making me walk deeper into the clearing.

I shrugged. "I don't know."

"Then think. Find it."

I looked around, searching not for the necklace, but for a solution. A way out of this.

My gaze landed on the fire pit and something, a force, wrapped around my heart and pulled hard. I sucked in a breath, but quickly turned around.

"You've seen something." Sean was in my face in one second flat. "Where is it?"

"I don't know."

His hand closed around my neck, and he pulled up, hurting me. "Hazel, I swear on my power, find the damn necklace or this won't be pretty."

"It's already not pretty," I said, my voice hoarse.

He growled at me. "Then how about this? I know Shade, Anna, and Britta are inside the castle right now, looking for you. If you don't find the necklace in the next thirty seconds, I'll kill them."

"They are stronger than you are." Truth was, I didn't know that. I had no idea of the extent of the sisters' or Sean's powers.

"I know that castle like no one else. I can lure them into a trap and attack them before they even know what is happening. They won't have time to react."

Deep inside my core, I knew Britta and Anna could kick Sean's ass if they were prepared for it. But if he tricked them, if he trapped them, I wasn't sure what could happen. I certainly didn't want the sisters hurting Sean, not permanently. Somehow, someday, I would find a way to bring him back to me, and I needed him intact for that.

"Untie me," I said, my tone flat.

Sean studied me for a moment. Deciding he could probably take me on—I didn't doubt it—he moved his fingers and the dark smoky rope evaporated.

Stilling myself, I walked toward the fire pit. I knelt in front of it, pulled most of the ivy and overgrown plant from its top, then placed my hand in the center. A quick zap of lightning and fire erupted inside it.

But it wasn't a normal fire. It was enchanted.

"Wait," Sean said from behind me. He put his hand on my shoulder.

And then we were in the past.

Prince Thales and I were seated on the stone bench, my head on his shoulder, his arm around my waist, and we looked at the magical fire crackling in front of us.

"So even if it was raining, it'll still burn?" he asked.

"Yes. Only I can extinguish it."

"What if we forget it's lit?"

"I enchanted it so it can't escape this pit and it can't burn anything, just provide warmth."

"Perfect." He kissed the top of my head. "Just like you."

"You spoil me."

"I wish I could do more."

"What you do, what you are, what we are ... it's enough."

I turned my face to his with a smile. Thales cupped my cheek and moved his lips to mine.

"Stop it," Sean said, bringing me back to the present. He took a step back and shook his head once. He had seen the memory too.

"I didn't do anything. The memories come without warning. You know that."

He stared at me, his eyes hard. "Just ... find the necklace."

I glanced at the fire. It was darker than a normal fire and every so often a strand of black flame sparked within.

I reached my hand inside the fire pit. Calling my magic,

I lifted the false bottom and immediately jumped back as a thick column of dark fire jutted to the sky. I tripped on the uneven stone path and started to go down—

"Careful!" Sean stepped behind me and wrapped a strong arm around my waist, pulling my back to his chest. I breathed hard from the unexpected fire, the almost falling, and now being on Sean's arms. Maybe he didn't notice it, but he still held on to me. "Did you know about that?"

I shook my head. "That wasn't my magic."

The column of fire disappeared and only my enchanted fire remained.

As if he had suddenly realized what he was doing, Sean pushed me away from him, but he didn't let me go until he knew I was steady on my feet.

He took a step back. "Hm, what could it be, then?"

I shrugged, approaching the fire pit again. "Anna and Britta built in lots of failsafes, lots of protection spells. I can only imagine this was their way of protecting the necklace in case someone found it other than them." They could at least have told me about it, couldn't they? I guess they thought we would find it together.

I thought so too.

I reached inside the fire pit, pushed aside the half-open false bottom. I patted the new bottom and found only a bed of small rocks. Frowning, I pushed the rocks aside, burying my hand in them. My shoulder was inside the fire pit when my fingertips brushed against something soft.

I couldn't help smiling as I reached down a little more and closed my hand around a small velvet pouch. I pulled it out and—

The scene from before continued in my head:

Behind me, Thales whispered, "I love you, Arianna. I love you like I never thought I could love anyone or anything." His lips grazed my jaw, and with a gasp, I leaned my head back on his shoulder. His hand traveled down, from my throat, past my collarbone, to the top curve of my breast. Agonizingly slow, he traced his fingers along my skin, dipping below my cleavage, and brushing his lips across my skin.

I turned my head to him, giving him access to my mouth; he captured them with hunger.

"I love you too, Thales," I whispered against his mouth. "Too much."

In an instant, Thales twirled me around, lowered me to the blanket in the grass, and leaned over me, his body a heavenly weight pressing against mine.

Then his mouth was on mine again, so eager, so hard, so perfect. His hand found the hem of my dress and slowly slid up my leg, and—

"That's enough." Sean snatched the pouch from my hands.

For a moment, I stood there. My hands shook as I took a deep breath to calm myself. Holy mother, that had been hot.

I swallowed hard and reached for the necklace. "Wait."

Retreating, Sean opened the pouch and turned it upside down above his hand. The necklace tumbled out of the pouch and we both halted, staring at it.

Holy shit, it was real. So real, I could feel the magic pulsing from inside the gem.

Closing his fingers around the necklace, Sean looked at

me, the black veins in his face darkening even more. "One down, two to go." He grabbed my wrist with his other hand. "Let's go."

I positioned myself in front of him. "Wait." I brought the arm he was holding up and rested my hand over his chest. My free hand, I placed over his closed palm.

I called on the magic within the necklace.

"No," he groaned, but the magic enveloped him, around us, trapping us in the eye of an invisible tornado of magic.

I closed my eyes and focused, first on the necklace's power, then on the darkness inside Sean. My senses dove into him, searching every corner of his being for the darkness, and I was shocked to find it everywhere. The darkness was deeply woven within every fiber, every muscle, every bone of his body.

A sob lodged in my throat. No, it didn't matter. Even if this was the hardest thing I had ever done, I would free him of it. I had to. I dug deeper, calling more of my power and the necklace's to fight against it.

Sean's groan became almost a shout. His knees folded and landed hard on the ground. I kept my grip on his chest and on his hand, even when his darkness pushed back, expanding inside of him, trying to push me away.

"Please, Sean," I whispered. "Come back to me."

"Hazel."

I glanced at him—the black eyes were gone, the dark lines faded away.

"You're back!" I dropped the magic. Sean embraced me,

burying his face on my neck. I melted in his arms. "I've missed you."

"Oh, Hazel." His chest shook, and at first, I thought he was either hurt or crying. Then I heard the soft laughter beside my ear. I pushed back and found him laughing at me. "You're so gullible."

"What?" It was all back. The paleness, the black eyes, the dark lines. He was still a demon. I retreated a full step. "How is this possible?"

He offered me a half grin. "All I had to do was give in to it for a few seconds. The moment I did, you eased your magic, and I took back the reins." He hooked his hand around the necklace and twirled it around his finger. "If you want the necklace, you'll do what I tell you."

"I don't think so!"

A white bolt zipped through the air and hit his forearm. Sean staggered back and the necklace fell to the ground.

Anna and Britta entered the clearing, magic sizzling in their hands. Shade appeared from the other side in cat form and snatched the necklace before Sean could. He pounced away.

"You," Sean said through gritted teeth.

"Back away or we'll fry you," Anna said as magic sparked stronger above her hand. Sean didn't move. She threw a couple of bolts at his feet, forcing him to move back a few feet. "You should be running."

Sean turned his glare to me. "This isn't over, my love."

Then he turned around and ran into the forest.

Anna and Britta rushed to me.

"Are you okay?" Britta asked while she scanned my face and Anna examined my body. "Did he hurt you?"

I shook my head. "I don't think he wanted to hurt me."

"Even that twisted version of him still loves you," Anna said.

"I think so," I admitted, my voice soft. Dejected.

Britta took hold of my elbow. "We should get out of here before he comes back."

"Or more dark witches show up." Anna pressed her lips into a thin line. "We found the bodies in the woods."

I stared at them both, tears coming to my eyes. "I killed one of them ... to save him."

"Oh, dear." Anna hugged me first, and Britta hugged the two of us. "I'm so sorry you had to do that."

"I promise we can talk more, dissect everything, and do so over a warm cup of tea or a glass of wine," Britta said, "but first, let's get out of here."

"Right." Anna took my hand in hers and guided me the opposite way Sean had run.

As we left the clearing, I couldn't help glancing back one more time.

But Sean was nowhere to be seen.

9

IN SILENCE, WE RAN THROUGH THE FOREST. WE DIDN'T EVEN bother going through the castle again. We skirted the outer wall until we reached the road back to the village. There were a few castle workers on our way, but Anna and Britta spelled them so they didn't see us.

We slowed down a bit when we reached the village, and we only stopped when we were inside my room at the hotel. Shade was there, in his human form, seated on his bed, with the necklace spread out beside him.

I froze, my eyes on the necklace, and I couldn't stop the avalanche of emotions from spilling out. A sob ripped past my throat and tears blurred my vision.

"Oh, Hazel." Anna embraced me. She patted my back and whispered, "Britta, order some tea."

"No." I pulled back and wiped at my eyes, though the tears didn't slow down. "We can't stay here. Sean can find me."

Britta frowned. "He won't be foolish enough to come

right now. Take a few minutes to calm down and process everything. Meanwhile, we'll order tea and pack to leave."

I glanced from Britta, to Anna, to Shade. None of them seemed keen in budging, so I plopped down on the bed and let the tears come.

By the time the tea arrived, Britta, Anna, and Shade had already packed all of our stuff—granted, it wasn't much.

Shade grabbed a steaming cup from the tray and gave it to me. "It's chamomile," he said. "It should help."

Anna stepped forward, wiggled her fingers above my cup, then offered me a tight smile. "Now it'll help even more."

I took a sip of tea. Its warmth spread through me like a cozy blanket, and I sighed. When I was done with half my cup, I finally told them all that had happened. How Shade and I got separate, how Sean was able to find us, that he had memories of his own, that I had killed for the first— and only—time to save him, and that I thought I could have reversed Catarina's spell with just the necklace.

"I was so stupid," I muttered.

"No, not stupid," Britta said. "But in love."

I scoffed. "Same difference."

"If Sean can find you, then we can't stay here," Shade said. He stood beside the packed bags, ready to go.

I nodded. "We won't be able to stay anywhere for long." I told them Sean knew we had spent a few days at the cottage outside New Orleans.

"We'll have to be on the move constantly until we can get him back." Anna stepped right in front of me. "But we can try something else." She moved her hands over my head, muttering something in Latin under her breath. A sprinkle of magic fell over me. "This should make it harder for him to sense you, at least for a while. It'll give us a head start."

"Thanks, by the way," I said. "For not hurting him back at the clearing. I know you could, I know you wanted to …"

"He's Prince Thales and your Sean," Britta said. "We won't hurt him unless he hurts you first."

I nodded, pushed up, and set my empty cup on the nightstand between the beds. I picked up the necklace and stared at it for a moment. I wasn't sure I could control the immense power inside it, but it was mine, so I put it on and tucked it under my sweater.

"We should go," I said, determined.

Without another word, everyone picked up their bags and we marched out of the room. In the lobby, Shade called for the valet to bring our car around.

We waited outside, at the round driveway in front of the hotel.

"Uh-oh." Anna stepped before me, her back to the street. "Brotherhood of Purity."

My stomach clenched. I spied around her shoulder—five men in red cloaks stood on the sidewalk across the street. They spoke to a young blond woman … who looked a lot like me.

"Shit. They are looking for me." I pulled the hood of my jacket up.

Shade nudged my arm. "You three go around the

corner and wait for me there. Hide inside a store if you have to. I'll bring the car to you."

Anna hooked her arm on mine, and keeping our backs to the street, we walked away from the hotel, the opposite way the members of the Brotherhood were.

As Shade suggested, we turned the corner and entered a small giftshop full of fake magic potions and spell books —not the best hiding place for three witches.

Anxious and tense, we pretended to browse for the next ten minutes, until finally, Shade texted us. A minute later, he stopped the car in front of the shop.

The sisters and I raced to the car, and as soon as the doors were closed, Shade peeled away, leaving dust behind us.

I glanced back, afraid the Brotherhood had seen us, but I couldn't see them anymore.

Relieved, I settled in the backseat and closed my eyes.

IT HADN'T BEEN MY INTENTION TO NAP.

Britta, who had been with me in the backseat, shook me awake. "We're here."

"Here where?" I rubbed the sleep from my eyes. It was dark out, and all I could see was the narrow road we were driving down. A few buildings lined the road—houses, a school, a couple of restaurants, and a hotel.

"In Terentia," Shade said as he took the hotel's driveway. "It's four hours from Venopolis."

I frowned. The sisters had told me they believed the

grimoire was in Venopolis. I glanced at my phone; it was almost midnight. "Wouldn't it be better if we pushed through to Venopolis, and got the grimoire?"

"After the day we had, I'm too tired to stay on the road for another five minutes." Shade stopped the car in one of the few open parking spots behind the hotel.

"I can drive, then," I said.

Britta gave me a side glance. "You woke up from a seven-hour deep sleep. You're probably still groggy and tired, despite the nap."

"I'm good." I rolled my shoulder, and then winced when something pulled at my neck. Shit. My body hurt all over, and yes, I had to admit, I was still tired. And yet, I didn't want to stop.

"It's okay, Hazel." Anna turned on the passenger seat and looked at me. "We'll stop only for a handful of hours, and we can take turns keeping watch."

I didn't like that.

"We can also cast some wards around the hotel," Britta suggested. "If someone gets close, we'll know."

Still not great, but I knew I wouldn't be able to fight them on this. I grunted as I opened the car's door and stepped out. It was a chilly November night, and I wished I had a thicker jacket to fight off the brutal late-fall wind.

We checked into two adjoining rooms. Shade offered to find dinner for us, while Anna, Britta, and I went outside to cast the wards.

The hotel sat on a big lot, with plenty of space around it. To the right, there was a two-story office building, to the left, a church, across the street was a diner and a laundry place. Behind it was a big open space with a sprinkling of trees and bushes, and farther behind it, we could see a tall fences and the back of houses.

I squinted my eyes against the dark night but didn't see anything suspicious as we walked the lot's perimeter and the sisters started on the wards.

"How do I do it?"

"Channel your magic, and go around chanting words that mean protection," Anna said. "Like *praesidium* and *protectio*."

"There are better ways to do this, make it more secure, but we don't have the time or the ingredients for those spells," Britta explained. She set off in the opposite way.

"Can I try?" I asked Anna.

"Sure." She gestured for me to take the lead.

I closed my eyes and inhaled, calling my magic. I felt it deep inside me and from the necklace—it pulsed under my sweater, the magic so alive, so powerful, so eager to be used.

I opened my mouth to start the chanting when a shudder coursed through my body and the wind suddenly felt colder.

"What was that?" I asked, looking around.

"I don't know." Anna took a step closer, as tense as I was.

We stared out into the open field behind the lot, but nothing was out there. Until there was. As if they had blinked into existence, a dozen Brotherhood of Purity members walked toward us.

Anna grabbed my hand and pulled me back. We

turned, stopping dead before we took one step. Britta was rushing our way as another handful of Brotherhood members closing in on her.

Suddenly, we were at the edge of the hotel's parking lot, surrounded by at least twenty of our enemies.

A tall man stepped forward. He lowered his hood, revealing a bald head and a face with sharp lines. "You must be Hazel," he said, looking at me. His voice was deep but raspy, and it rubbed me the wrong way. "Our Brothers in America have been looking for you."

I wondered if they knew why, if they too were after my necklace, my grimoire, and my ashes. I wouldn't dare ask, though.

Anna and Britta flanked me, their magic ready and under their skin. I inhaled deeply, making sure mine was ready too.

"What do we do?" I asked, my voice low.

"Fight," Anna answered. "Is there another option?"

No, there wasn't.

Though they were twenty against three, we had magic and they didn't. My stomach revolved with the idea of hurting or killing someone. Maybe I could stun them while we escaped.

"I advise you to surrender and make it easy for everyone," the man said. He tilted his head. "Do you need time to think? I can give you ..." He pretended to look at nonexistent watch on his wrist. "Three seconds. One, two ... get them!"

The Brotherhood members surged forward, pulling their weapons from under their cloaks. Anna and Britta acted on instinct, throwing bolts of magic, and creating barriers to stop them but the swarm came from all sides.

I dug deep inside of me and called my lightning. The night turned inky black and crackling came from my hands. I lifted my arms and dark lightning descended from the sky. The Brotherhood members shouted as they scurried to get out of the way.

"Clever," the bald man said. Then he placed a small metal box on the ground and pressed a button on its top.

A hum started, piercing my ears in the most painful way. My magic failed and the Brotherhood advanced. I gritted my teeth, endured the pain, and threw more lightning at them.

Only, I barely had any power left. The lightning crackled at my fingertips but died as soon as it left my hands.

I stared at my palms, confused. Beside me, Anna and Britta tried throwing bolts at our enemies, but they too couldn't.

"What's happening?" Britta asked, extending her arm once more and watching as nothing came out.

"It's that device," I said, pointing to the metal box. "Somehow, it's messing with our magic."

"And killing my ears," Anna said.

The bald man pressed the button again and the hum increased. Britta, Anna, and I clamped our ears and shouted in terrible pain. I fell to my knees as the pain spread, feeling like a hand squeezing every inch of my head, my throat, and my chest.

A boom sounded and the hum stopped.

Panting, I lowered my arms and glanced around.

Sean rushed the Brotherhood, moving like a ninja. Almost too fast to follow, he grabbed the neck of a man, snapped it, then he placed his hand on the chest of another, and the man fell on the ground as if his heart had stopped, then Sean enveloped a man in a tornado of darkness, and we heard his gasp for the air that left him.

In the middle of it all, the metal box smoked.

For a brief moment, Sean stopped. He looked at me with his dark, angry eyes. "I'll take care of them. Go."

I blinked. What? He was helping us?

Anna and Britta didn't care what his reasons were. They grabbed my arms and ran toward the front of the hotel, carrying me along with them. Sean continued the carnage, killing each Brotherhood member as if they were flies on the wall.

The squeal of wheels cut through the air and a car drifted to a stop beside us.

Shade looked at us from the window. "Get in!"

We piled inside the car, almost smashing the dinner he had bought, and he stepped on the gas, wheels squealing.

I glanced back, but from here I couldn't see anything but the front of the hotel and the rest of the street. I sat back in the seat, my insides still sore from that metal box, and my heart racing.

"Was that Sean?" Shade asked.

"Yes," Anna answered. She was seated beside me in the backseat. "How did you know to get a car?"

This was not the car we had rented when we first arrived in Germany.

"I was arriving at the hotel with our food when I heard the confusion in the back," he explained as he continued driving fast, leaving the town behind. "Our car was back there, so I had no choice."

"Thank you," Britta said. "You arrived just in time."

"Our things are in the hotel, though," he said, his voice tight.

"We can come back later and get it all," Anna said. "Maybe." She looked at me. "Are you okay? Did they hurt you?"

I glanced at her. "I don't think so." My voice was low, strained.

"I think whatever you did before, in the clearing, with the necklace, might have worked, in a way."

My brows knotted. "What do you mean?"

She shrugged. "I don't know, it's just ... I don't think Sean would have saved the day that way before. I think he would have found a way to get in there, get you, and leave Britta and me to die."

Britta twisted on her seat and looked at me. "I agree. Maybe, it's just like with your powers and your memories. They are coming slowly, in batches."

Which meant that if we gave him time, perhaps Sean would come back on his own? That was a crazy theory, one we didn't have time to test.

"Maybe." I turned toward the window and stared at the vast darkness outside.

After a few silent minutes, Shade asked, "What now?"

"We can't stop," Britta said. "Just drive."

10

WE STOPPED TWICE. WE HAD BEEN ON THE GO FOR TOO long, and we needed rest and food. Each time we stopped at a gas station, where we filled up the car, used the bathroom, got some food, and then parked out of sight for about twenty to thirty minutes. Each time, one of us stayed up while the others slept. First, it was Anna, then it was Britta. I had argued I wanted to keep watch too, but the sisters weren't having it, and I wouldn't waste the little sleep I could get.

It didn't come easy, though. My mind and my body were wound up, and the sight of Sean saving us flashed in my mind each time I closed my eyes.

Why had he done that? What did it mean?

When I eventually fell asleep, I had only a few minutes until it was time to go. Thankfully, Shade insisted on driving, and I napped in the backseat.

One other thing that kept popping in my mind nonstop: It had been more than twenty-four hours since I had last had a shower, probably over thirty, and I really wanted to wash my hair! It was silly but come on! Who wanted to fight evil with dirty hair and smelly clothes?

"We're here," Shade announced, and we all sat up in the car.

I opened my eyes and closed them because of the bright sunlight. Shit, Shade must have been driving for hours, and we all slept instead of keeping him company.

"We haven't been here in centuries," Anna said, her voice holding a sad tone.

I glanced around the small village—narrow cobblestone streets, two- and three-story buildings, ivy and flowers taggling over the stone walls. Tiny cars and vespas drove the twisted streets, and people walked by, coming in and out of shops and houses. In front of restaurants and cafes, small foldable tables and chairs took up half the street, making it impossible to cross.

"Where are we?" I asked.

"A small Italian village," Britta answered.

"It was even smaller when we lived here," Anna said.

I frowned. "You lived here?"

Anna nodded. "After Prince Thales died, we hid for a while."

"We weren't hiding," Britta added. "We were recouping. Getting stronger. Coming up with a better plan."

"Right," Anna said. "So, we bought a house here."

"Far away from Grandisia."

Britta sighed. "That didn't seem to matter. It took the Brotherhood a couple of years to find us."

My eyes widened. "They found you here?"

"You'll see," Anna said, sad.

The buildings grew apart as we drove. Another block or so, and some even had a small front and side yard.

Shade stopped the car in front of a condemned house —a narrow stone building of three stories that had been shattered by fire. Only one side of the walls stood tall, the rest seemed to have crumbled down. The stones and brick-work lay blackened.

"What happened here?" I asked, confused.

"The Brotherhood found us." Anna opened the car's door. "And they did this."

I exited the car, confused. "But ... wasn't that centuries ago?" By now, this house should have been restored, or torn apart, or rebuilt.

"It's still ours," Britta said. We all stood on the sidewalk, in front of the open gates—one iron gate was on the ground, the other was twisted, and both seemed like they would crumble to dust if we touched them.

I snapped my gaze to them. "Why?"

Anna shrugged. "We're attached to it, I guess."

"We came here alone and wounded." Britta's eyes filled with tears. "Our coven was practically gone, and we had no hope. This is where we started over, where we came up with our plans, where we started executing them."

The sisters joined hands and my heart squeezed for them.

Shade cleared his throat. "You weren't alone."

"You were just a normal familiar," Anna said. "But yeah, it was here we made you human."

Suddenly, I wanted restore this house. Being over seven

hundred years old, it would probably be really outdated, but we could do some improvements without taking from the original plan.

I shook my head. What the hell was I thinking?

"And you think the grimoire is here?" I asked.

"That's what the rune suggested," Anna said."

"It makes sense because this is where we last saw it," Britta said. "We thought we had hidden it and it hadn't been destroyed by the fire. But when we came back later to retrieve it, we couldn't find it."

"We assumed the Brotherhood had taken it during the surprise attack," Anna added. "Recently we learned they had been after the book."

"That coincided with when we learned you had come back to life," Britta said. "After you showed us the runes, I wondered if the book has some kind of spell to protect itself." She looked at me. "Ring any bells?"

I frowned, raking my memories, but nothing came to mind. I didn't even remember what my grimoire looked like.

An older woman with a blue bandana over her gray hair walked behind us. She clutched her reusable bag closer to herself as she kept stealing glances at us.

Finally, after a few more steps, she stopped, turned to us, and said something in Italian.

Anna replied, and I was shocked to hear the southern Italian accent in her voice as if she was a native. The older woman didn't seem happy, but Anna remained calm and respectful.

After a few exchanges, the older woman grumbled and walked away.

"What was that about?" I asked, curious.

"The woman wanted to know why we're looking at the house," Shade answered.

I blinked at him. He also knew Italian? I was the only here who didn't? Well, they were all over seven hundred years old. They probably spoke a lot more languages.

"Yes, she asked if we know the owners." Britta smiled, amused. "She said the town has been trying to contact the owners for years. They don't like how the house has been left like this for centuries."

"It makes the entire town look ugly," Anna said. "Her words, not mine." She shook her head and started forward.

"She also said that two people died inside the house a week ago," Shade said. "Not on the same day, but the same way."

I gulped. "How?"

He stared at me. "As if their life had been sucked from the inside out."

"What does that mean?"

"That we might have some kind of ghost living in this house." Britta looked at me. "Do you still have the hawthorn berry powder?"

I outstretched my arms. "I've got nothing." All our things were left at the inn and I hadn't brought any ingredients for spells on this trip.

"We'll find another way to free it, then." Anna nodded. "Anyway, we're wasting precious time. Shall we?"

"So ..." I followed, careful where I stepped. The short

pathway from the gate to the front porch was littered with stones, pieces of metal and wood, and overgrown plants. "We go around the rubble and search for the book?"

"Basically." Anna toed the porch steps, before fully stepping on them. They creaked loudly, and for a moment, we went still. "Though, if we're right, you'll be the only one able to find it."

Great.

Taking a long breath, I stepped on the flimsy porch and ducked under a heavy beam that had fallen by the front door—which was broken in half, and what was left was charred to a crisp.

The moment my foot stepped inside the house, a veil of cold covered me. "Everyone is feeling this?"

"Yes," came from the three of them.

"It's the ghost," Anna said. "It could be anywhere."

I took careful steps toward the center of the house, right where a wide hallway and a large staircase were located. I focused and sent my senses in a wide arc around me. Usually, I was able to sense ghosts, their energy, but this time, I felt nothing.

I channeled my magic and whispered, "*Apparet.*"

Nothing happened.

Shade went off to the left, Anna went to the right, and Britta braved the half-gone stairs.

As I walked around the big house, I searched for the ghost and the grimoire, my senses wide open, my magic at my fingertips.

Anna appeared at my side. "Maybe the ghost is downstairs."

I turned to her. "Downstairs?"

"Yes, there are two stories below us." She gestured for me to follow her. "The door should be right here." We rounded the stairs, until a stone wall that despite charred, still stood the test of time. "Under here."

She waved her hand and several of the big stones at the bottom moved away, revealing a small opening.

"There used to be a door there," Britta said, coming from behind us. Shade was right beside her. She glanced at the dark hole beyond the door. "And stairs."

Shade shifted into his cat form and jumped into the hole. After a few seconds, his voice came from below. "It's just the first three steps missing. The others are broken, but you can make it."

Anna was the first to sit down on the floor and scoot to the hole. Holding on to the stones—the only sound structure in the house—she lowered herself into the hole.

Britta pointed to the opening. "Your turn."

Awesome. Blowing out a breath, I copied Anna. For a second, when lowering myself and not finding any steps, I panicked, but then a hand grasped my foot and guided it to the weak wood. Slowly, I descended the rest of the stairs and immediately held my breath. The smell was terrible—a mix of mold, rust, burnt wood, and decay.

Anna had cast several bolts of white light to float around, illuminating everything. This first level was mostly one big, open room, the ceiling high, and I could see the remains of where tables and shelves stood. This was probably where they practiced magic, made potions, and kept their grimoires and other books.

A squeak came from a corner, and I almost jumped. A rat scurried under a broken shelf and disappeared into the darkness. When inspecting the shelves closer, I saw plenty of cockroaches hiding among them.

I shuddered, wishing I could be anywhere but here. "Where did you keep my grimoire?"

"On the next level," Britta said as she walked down the steps and moved behind it. She grabbed a metal handle from the floor and pulled. The black trap door broke from its rusty hinges, and she discarded it. "It's not like we needed it."

A clicking sound echoed through the room and we all stopped.

"That doesn't sound like a rat," I said.

"Nor a ghost," Shade said.

Slowly, we turned to the sound ... someone crouched in a dark corner. Anna's lights floated closer, and I stilled. The woman had gray skin and long dark hair. Her limbs were sickly thin, and she had dark veins all over.

The clicking sound came again, as she turned her face and stared at us. I took a step back, my heart going a mile an hour—she had deep yellow eyes, wide black lips, and razor-sharp teeth that snapped and clicked together.

It was straight out of a horror movie.

"She's not a ghost," Britta said, her voice low.

Footsteps sounded from above us. The woman shrieked and ran to another dark corner.

Anna, Britta, and I prepared to fight the woman and whoever was upstairs. Then two people jumped down the hole and stood in front of us.

They raised their swords high above their heads, a green shine to the dark blade. Anna, Britta, and Shade turned to them, ready to attack.

"Wait!" I called out. Everyone froze. "You're ... Blackthorn Hunters."

The man, a tall guy with dirty blond hair, lowered his sword and narrowed his eyes at me. "Do we know you?" He had a deep English accent.

"No, but I know Norah and Doreen," I said.

"Ah," the dark-haired woman said. She seemed to relax a little. "From the Colorado Outpost." And she had a clear French accent. "That's on the other side of the pond."

"Yeah, we came this way for a mission," I said. Norah and Doreen seemed to live on missions, maybe these two would understand that.

"Ah, I see. We're from the Rome outpost," the guy answered. "I'm Peter and this is Monica."

"I'm Hazel." I pointed out the others and introduced them. "We're witches, and he's my familiar."

"A familiar who can shapeshift?" Peter asked, his brows raised. "That's new."

"As nice as it is to meet new supernaturals, and not have to instantly kill them," Monica said. "We're here on a mission of our own. We're hunting a demon who killed two people last week. She looks like those horror movie monsters. Have you seen her?"

Shade pointed to the far corner in the room. "She went that way."

Careful, the Blackthorn Hunters walked forward, and the rest of us stayed put, watching them attentively. Anna projected her lights to get a little closer, illuminating just enough without startling the demon.

There she was, in another corner, crouched down, with a rat in her hands. She took a bite out of the rat and munched with a gaping mouth, blood tricking down her chin, and hissed at the hunters.

My stomach revolved and I thought I would throw up.

When Peter lunged for her, the demon threw the half-eaten rat at him and crawled up the walls. But Monica knew what to expect. She found a broken wall and stood on top, reaching for the demon. It shrieked again and scurried off in our direction.

In a panic, I raised my hand and zapped it with lightning.

The demon fell to the ground with a heavy thud, writhing and wailing. Peter stepped to it and cut off its head.

The body stopped moving instantly.

And I turned away, sure I would throw up.

"Thanks," Monica said. I dared glance over my shoulder and saw Peter picking up the demon's body as if it was a limp noddle. "We have been chasing her for weeks now. Last night, we heard she might have come here."

I pressed a hand to my stomach. "Glad we could help."

She looked around. "Do you need help?"

"No, we're good," Anna said quickly.

Monica narrowed her eyes. "All right. Take care."

She helped Peter carry the demon's body and severed head up the broken stairs, and in another minute, they were both gone.

"That was ... something," Britta said. She glanced at me. "You've met Blackthorn Hunters recently?"

I nodded. "Why? Have I met them before?"

"Long ago, you met their founder, Randall," Anna said. "He wanted your help with a quest of his, but you had other troubles."

I frowned. "I don't remember that."

"This was fun and all, but we're wasting time," Shade reminded us.

"Right." I straightened and turned to the stairs. "Let's keep moving."

THE STAIRS LED TO A SMALL ROOM WITH STONE WALLS marked by the fire.

I turned in a circle, confused. "This is it?"

Anna shook her head. "Don't you know us by now?"

She and Britta touched a stone in the middle of the wall behind the stairs. "*Aperta*," they said together, and then stepped back.

Like pieces of a magical puzzle, the stone moved to the side, creating an opening big enough for an average height witch. Anna, Britta, and I walked through the archway, the floating lights following us. Shade had to duck and twist his shoulders to get through.

Anna's lights spread through the room, and I halted, staring at it in amazement.

This place was a copy of the upstairs room, but bigger, with more shelves, more books, more tables, more tools, and less destroyed by the fire.

And right in the center, was a narrow, tall table, almost like a pedestal.

"It seems the Brotherhood didn't get to this room when they attacked you," I said, walking toward the pedestal.

"That's what we thought too," Britta said. She had approached a tall shelf to my right and gestured to the fallen books and empty spaces. "But the room was a mess, and our grimoires were gone, along with so many other books."

"Some of our most precious and rare ingredients were gone too," Anna continued. She stood before a long table to my left, where broken vials, pestle and mortars, and stools were in a heap. "If it wasn't them, then someone else got in here and stole everything."

"Including your grimoire," Britta said.

"But ..." I stopped in front of the pedestal. "If my grimoire isn't here, then why would the runes point us to this place?" After all, the runes hadn't been wrong about the necklace.

Anna sighed. "I don't know."

"Whatever we're here to do, we should do it fast," Shade reminded us. "It's only a matter of time until we're found."

By Sean.

Honestly, as much as I wanted Sean back, I wasn't keen on meeting evil Sean anytime soon.

I shuddered and stared at the pedestal. "Is this where my grimoire stood?" It was still so odd to think that something of mine had been so important, it had its own special place.

"Yes," Britta said.

I placed my hands on top of the smooth surface, closed my eyes, and focused. My magic hummed underneath my skin, eager to be used. Something pushed against me, a force, a power I knew.

"I can feel it." I opened my eyes. "It's here."

The sisters walked closer to me.

"How?" Anna asked. "We searched this place before."

"We even used magic and we couldn't find it," Britta said.

"It's probably because it didn't want to be found," I whispered. "Until now." I called my magic. The blue pendant shone and lightning cut from the ceiling, striking the pedestal, right between my hands.

Smoke rose and a burnt smell filled my nostrils.

The pedestal crumbled into shiny dust, and something shimmered into existence right into my palms.

My grimoire.

With a gasp, I gripped it tight.

I was in the castle's library, writing a spell in my grimoire. I had several new spells come to me in the past few days, and I couldn't stop writing them.

Anna, Britta, and Jewell sat around me, working on their grimoires, while several other books were piled high on the long table—all about herbs, crystals, and magic. Books that until a few months ago had been nonexistent in this library, but now were held in a locked section.

Footsteps echoed down the hallway outside, and I stilled.

Prince Thales, dressed in his dark blue uniform, entered the library, his sword hanging from his hip. Two other soldiers flanked him.

The girls and I rose and curtsied at his presence.

"Arianna, come with me," he said, his voice tight. He barely met my eyes.

My stomach sank. "A-am I in trouble?"

He frowned and for a moment I thought he wouldn't answer me. "I think my father has a job for you."

"Oh." I looked at the girls. They nodded in anticipation. The king's approval of our activities was important, and working on his quests was how we kept on his good side.

"Follow me." He turned and marched out of the room.

I scurried to follow him.

"Always so serious," Jewell said, her voice low.

"I'm sure he likes Arianna," that was Britta.

"I agree," Anna said. "And he's fighting it."

A thrill coursed through my body. Did he like me? No ... I had saved his sister a couple of months ago and had been working with him here and there since then. He barely knew me. He couldn't like me.

Could he?

I sped up, trying to keep up with his long steps.

I blinked and stared at the book in my hands. It was like I had imagined, but more. A thick, heavy leather-bound tome with golden, yellowed pages, and a thick golden embroidery on the cover—the rune for truth.

A rush of magic coursed from the grimoire to me, and I inhaled deeply. Knowledge filled my mind, and I was sure I had over half of my memories back, along with my magic.

I smiled at Anna, Britta, and Shade. "I would say I'm about sixty, sixty-five percent myself."

The sisters embraced me, and Shade winked at me from several steps back. I stretched my arm and pulled him to us. "Come here, furball."

He groaned but relented and hugged us back. I hadn't known him as a human, but now I remembered him as a cat, and we had been inseparable. He had been more than a pet, he had been like a brother, a family member, my best friend.

"That's so touching," a voice said. We all turned to the entrance, where Sean stood, a smug grin on his lips. His dark eyes landed on the book in my hands. "I see you found it. Well done."

Anna poked me on the back, and somehow, I knew what she meant. She, Britta, and Shade took several steps to the side.

Sean's shadows twirled around him. "Stay where you are."

They stopped, but I drew Sean's attention back to me. "Are you going to try and take it?" I hugged the grimoire. "And the necklace too?"

He tilted his head. "I should probably wait for you to find your ashes too, but I'm eager to get this show going." He jerked his chin once. "Come with me."

I shook my head. "I'm not going anywhere with you, Sean."

He growled, baring his teeth. "Don't make this difficult, Hazel. I know you don't want to hurt me, but I have no qualms about hurting your friends." He moved his hand toward Britta and a wave of darkness flew her way.

She ducked under a table and scurried farther to the side. "You missed!" she taunted him.

Sean took two steps closer. "You all know you'll lose."

"Want to bet?" Anna threw a small bolt at his side. To avoid it, Sean twisted and moved deeper into the room.

"You're getting on my nerves," he hissed.

In cat form, Shade jumped on Sean's back. Sean doubled over and almost fell forward, and Shade jumped out of the way, before Sean could do anything.

Sean fumed. "What the—" A hum echoed in the room. "What's that?"

Anna walked forward and pointed to the faint circle drawn near the room's entrance. "You're trapped."

With a growl, Sean summoned his darkness and flung it at us—but the tendrils bumped into an invisible wall and faded like smoke. He pushed against it with his bare hands, but there was no budging. This circle had been drawn almost seven hundred years ago by Britta and Anna. There was no breaking it.

My eyes on Sean, I opened my grimoire to the exact page I wanted and let go of it. The grimoire floated in the air before me. Anna and Britta stepped to my side and held my hands.

Together, we read the enchantment. "*Accipere tenebra auferet.*"

It literally read *take this darkness away*. We had come up with this spell long ago, when something similar happened to the people of our village. The details were hazy in my mind, but I remembered saving them all.

The necklace warmed against my skin as I pulled from its magic. The circle's line shone bright as the magic enveloped Sean.

"No!" he shouted. "Don't do this!"

Lightning struck around the circle. Sean crumbled to his knees, groaning as the magic penetrated his body, his soul, and pursued the darkness within.

My heart squeezed at the sight, but I knew it had to be done.

"*Accipere tenebra auferet,*" I repeated nonstop, putting more of my power into my words, into the spell, into my intention. I didn't care as long as it worked.

With a whimper, Sean's body fell forward. A moment later, a dark cloud rose from his back, until it faded near the ceiling.

Anna, Britta, and I let the magic go. The lightning stopped; the circle lost its shine. The room was silent for a few seconds, the only sound the hard beating of my heart.

"Is it done?" Shade asked.

"I—I think so." I started forward.

Shade lifted his finger. "Stay back. I'll check him. If anything happens, lock the both of us in the circle."

"But—"

He stomped inside the circle and knelt beside Sean. "Hey." He touched Sean's shoulder. "Sean? Wake up." He pressed two fingers to Sean's neck, and I held my breath. Three seconds later, Shade nodded. "He's alive."

I let out a long, relieved sigh.

Sean groaned and turned to the side. Shade scooted back, ready to jump and run or fight, if needed. Sean sat up and looked around, confused. My heart skipped a beat. His skin wasn't as pale as before, his eyes weren't black, and there were no dark lines around his eyes.

His eyes found mine, a knot between his eyes. "W-what happened?"

A sob tore through my throat and I made for him.

Britta caught my wrist and tugged me back. "Wait." She narrowed her eyes. "Sean, what do you remember?"

For a moment, he seemed lost. Then he looked at his hands, his eyes wide. "I remember ... I remember everything."

"And the darkness is gone?" Anna asked.

Sean stood and nodded; the frown came back. "It's gone." He stared at me, his eyes sad. "I'm back."

This time, when I ran to him, no one stopped me. I threw myself at him, and he almost fell back with the impact. His arms wrapped around me, and he buried his face in my neck.

"Thank the light," I whispered.

"No, thanks to you," he said, his voice equally low.

I pulled back and looked into his eyes. Before, at the castle, he had tricked me. I had to make sure that this time, it was him.

One corner of his lips tugged up, but it didn't seem happy. "It's really me, Hazel. I'm here."

I pulled him to me again. "Good. This time, I'm never letting you go."

CONTINUE READING HAZEL'S ADVENTURES WITH BOOK 6, *The Midnight Wish*!

BONUS: want to read an exclusive scene from Sean's POV? Download it here!

To read a special and exclusive book about another light witch, join my Facebook Group and find the book called *The Light Witch* to download on the "featured" tab!

THANK YOU

who finds out she's a demon hunter, and the half-demon intent on protecting her against all evil.

The Vampire Heir (Rite World 1: Rite of the Vampire): a dark and mysterious paranormal romance about a vampire and a young woman with a secret.

The Warlock Lord (Rite World 4: Rite of the Warlock): a thrilling and kick-ass paranormal romance about a were-wolf and warlock.

The Wolf Forsaken (Rite World 7: Rite of the Wolf): a heat-wrenching tale about a lost wolf shifter and a fae princess on the run.

Heart Seeker (The Fire Heart Chronicles book 1): an urban fantasy series about a young woman who finds herself at the center of a mysterious supernatural world.

Destiny Gift (The Everlast Series book 1): a post-apocalyptic urban fantasy series about a young woman with a special power that can save the world.

DON'T FORGET TO SIGN UP FOR MY NEWSLETTER TO FIND OUT about new releases, cover reveals, giveaways, and more!

If you want to see exclusive teasers, help me decide on covers, read excerpts, talk about books, etc, join my reader group on Facebook: Juliana's Club!

ABOUT THE AUTHOR

While USA Today Bestselling Author Juliana Haygert dreams of being Wonder Woman, Buffy, or a blood elf shadow priest, she settles for the less exciting—but equally gratifying—life as a wife, a mother, and an author. She resides in North Carolina and spends her days writing about kick-ass heroines and the heroes who drive them crazy.

Subscribe to her mailing list to receive emails of announcement, events, and other fun stuff related to her writing and her books: www.bit.ly/JuHNL

For more information:
www.julianahaygert.com

facebook.com/julianahaygert

twitter.com/julianahaygert

instagram.com/juliana.haygert

goodreads.com/juliana_haygert

pinterest.com/julianahaygert

bookbub.com/authors/juliana-haygert

youtube.com/julianahaygert

tiktok.com/@julianahaygert

ALSO BY JULIANA HAYGERT

To find links and more info, go to:
www.julianahaygert.com/books/

Shorts
Into the Darkest Fire

Standalones
Daughter of Darkness

Rite World: Night Wolves
The Night Calling (Book 1)
The Night Burning (Book 2)
The Night Hunting (Book 3)
The Night Rising (Book 4)

Rite World: Vampire Wars
The Darkest Vampire (Book 1)
The Darkest Witch (Book 2)
The Darkest Magic (Book 3)

Rite World: Lightgrove Witches
The Midnight Test (Book 1)
The Midnight Spell (Book 2)
The Midnight Flame (Book 3)
The Midnight Secret (Book 4)
The Midnight Hunt (Book 5)
The Midnight Wish (book 6)

Rite World: Blackthorn Hunters Academy
The Demon Kiss (Book 1)

The Hunter Secret (Book 2)
The Soul Bond (Book 3)
The Shadow Trials (Book 4)
The Infernal Curse (Book 5)

Rite World
The Vampire Heir (Book 1)
The Witch Queen (Book 2)
The Immortal Vow (Book 3)
The Warlock Lord (Book 4)
The Wolf Consort (Book 5)
The Crystal Rose (Book 6)
The Wolf Forsaken (Book 7)
The Fae Bound (Book 8)
The Blood Pact (Book 9)

The Wyth Courts
Winter King (Book 1)
Spring Warrior (Book 2)
Summer Prince (Book 3)
Autumn Rebel (Book 4)

The Fire Heart Chronicles
Heart Seeker (Book 1)
Flame Caster (Book 2)
Earth Shaker (Book 2.5)
Sorrow Bringer (Book 3)
Soul Wanderer (Book 4)
Fate Summoner (Book 5)
War Maiden (Book 6)

The Everlast Series
Destiny Gift (Book 1)
Soul Oath (Book 2)
Cup of Life (Book 3)
Everlasting Circle (Book 4)

<u>*Willow Harbor Series*</u>
Hunter's Revenge (Book 3)
Siren's Song (Book 5)

<u>*Breaking Series*</u>
Breaking Free (Book 1)
Breaking Away (Book 2)
Breaking Through (Book 3)
Breaking Down (Book 4)